In Thought, Word and Deed

by

James Parr

This is a work of fiction. Names, characters, places and incidents either are products of the author's imagination or are used fictitiously. Any resemblance to actual events or locales or persons, living or dead, is entirely coincidental.

Text copyright©2017 James Parr

All rights reserved

'I confess to almighty God, and to you, my brothers and sisters, that I have greatly sinned in my thoughts and in my words, in what I have done, and in what I have failed to do; through my fault, through my fault, through my most grievous fault. Therefore, I ask blessed Mary, ever virgin, all the angels and saints, and you, my brothers and sisters, to pray for me to the Lord our God.'

(Confiteor English translation)

Chapter One

'Dad, are you awake?'

Emma Woodbridge knocked gently on her father's door.

'Hello. Yes, come in.'

As she entered, Patrick Meyer switched on the bedside light and sat up.

'Hi Dad.' He was still on his own side of the bed and not in the centre, as she would have expected by now. She leaned over and kissed him 'Happy Christmas.'

'And a happy Christmas to you, my darling.'

'I've brought you a cup of tea.'

'Ah, now you're spoiling me. Are the others awake yet?'

'Jim's at his laptop. No sign of life from Sam and Zoe. Hardly surprising considering what they got through last night. And Zoe was already the worse for drink when they arrived.'

Patrick laughed. 'Nice girl though. I like her.'

'Very different from Saskia.'

'Very. But your brother's old enough by now to know what he's doing.'

Emma drew back the curtains and returned to his bedside. 'I'm going to Mass, Dad. Care to come?'

Patrick shook his head. 'I don't think so. Won't Jim go with you?'

'Only if I press him. Not to worry. I'm happy to go on my own. I want to visit Mum's grave.'

Patrick took his daughter's hand. 'Now, Emma, I don't want any brooding. It's good of you to come home for Christmas, but I want this to be a happy occasion. It's what your mother would have wanted.'

'I know...and it will be.' Emma felt her eyes moistening.

'I mean it, Em. We have to make the best of things. It's what I'm doing and so must you.'

She picked up the tray. 'No need to get up yet. I'll put out some cereals and people can breakfast when they're ready.'

Leaving her father's room she crossed the landing to her own bedroom. Jim was sitting up in bed working at his laptop.

'I've brought you some tea.'

'Thanks.'

You know what day it is, I assume.'

Looking up he stared blankly at her. 'Oh, yes. Happy Christmas.'

'So much for our night of passion.'

'He looked down sheepishly. 'Sorry. A glass or two too many I'm afraid.'

Emma took off her dressing gown and began to dress. 'I take it you still want this baby. You're not just stringing me along.'

'Of course I do,' he said, his fingers still hovering over the keyboard. 'We'll go to bed early tonight. Okay?'

She looked at him angrily. 'I hope you're not going to spend the whole of Christmas at that thing.'

'No. I just have to get this out of the way and then I'm done.'

'Well, I'm going to church. If you want to come you need to get up now. I don't want to be standing at the back.'

Emma made her way downstairs and set about gathering up wine glasses and empty bottles from the sitting room. Last night hadn't gone well. Dad put on a brave show of cheerfulness, as she knew he would, but Sam's behaviour was beyond the pale. What was he thinking of, inviting his new girlfriend home for Christmas? It must have occurred to him that Dad would still be feeling emotional so soon after Mum's death. He'd texted to say they would arrive by 7.30pm and she prepared the meal on that basis. By 8.15pm they still hadn't arrived and nor was he answering his phone. They breezed in eventually at 9.45pm with the excuse that Zoe had to stay behind at the salon for a Christmas drink.

Washing and drying the glasses she carried them back to the sitting room. So, Zoe was a hairdresser. Quite a change from Saskia then. Not that she had anything against hairdressers, but this one seemed such an airhead. Pretty though - there was no denying that. Flouncing around in that miniskirt, Dad couldn't take his eyes off her. Even Jim was showing a flicker of interest by the end of the evening.

'Good morning, sister.' Sam appeared, still in his dressing gown. 'I might have known it would be you making all that din.'

Emma took plates and mugs from the cupboard and began setting the table. 'Well, someone has to get the house straight.' She moved past him to open the cutlery drawer.

'Why are you down so early?'

'I'm going to Mass.'

'Ah, yes. You're still one of the obedient faithful, aren't you. Is Jim going?'

'Probably not.'

'Zoe will go with you. I doubt she's ever seen the inside of a church. It will be a new experience for her.'

Emma snorted derisively. 'I'd be surprised if Zoe manages to surface by lunchtime, judging by the state she was in last night?'

Sam smiled. 'Yes, she was a bit over the top. But that's our Zoe for you. Don't worry she'll be right as rain this morning.'

She looked at him sternly. 'Are you going to ring Saskia?'

'What? Give me a chance. I doubt she's even awake yet.'

'No, but Tommy will be. You should call him even if you don't want to talk to Saskia. And I assume you'll be going over to see him.'

'All right, Em. All in good time.' Sam reached into the cornflakes packet and took out a handful which he stuffed into his mouth.

'Oh... you're up.' A bleary eyed Zoe stumbled into the dining room. Without make up she looked even younger than her twenty years. 'Sorry. I thought it would just be Sam downstairs.'

Emma gave her a taut smile. 'Good morning, Zoe and a happy Christmas.'

'Yes, happy Christmas, Emma.' She sidled up to Sam and clung to his arm. 'But here you are, dressed already and I haven't even got my face on.'

'There's Alka Seltzer in the bathroom if you need it. Sam will get it for you, won't you Sam.'

Zoe sat down at the table, her head in her hands. 'Guys, I'm really sorry about last night. We'd been so busy all day that I barely had time for a sandwich. Then Anton said he wanted to take us all to the pub. And I was so looking forward to meeting you. Sam has told me so much about you.'

'Has he now? Well, I wouldn't give too much credence to what Sam has to say.'

'Don't worry about my little sister,' said Sam, pouring orange juice into a glass and giving it to Zoe. 'She can be a bit sharp but she has a heart of gold underneath.'

Now Patrick appeared, also in his dressing gown. 'Hello. Am I the last?' He looked round him. 'No. Still Jim to make an entry. Good morning, Zoe, and how are you feeling this morning?'

'I'm fine thank you, Mr Meyer, but I want to apologise for last night…'

'Nonsense. Bucks Fizz, that's what you need,' said Patrick opening the fridge door. 'And please, the name's Patrick. We don't stand on ceremony here.'

'Dad!' said Emma, intercepting him. 'The champagne's for later, when we open our presents.'

'Ah, yes, of course. Sorry, Zoe. You'll have to make do with orange juice'

'Well, someone has to think of these things,' said Emma. 'And I hope you've brought the wine I asked you to get, Sam.'

Sam stared at Emma. 'You didn't ask me to bring any wine.'

'I did! You know I did. I sent you an email listing exactly what to get. Don't tell me you didn't see it.'

He grinned. 'Okay, just teasing. It's in the boot. I'll bring it in while you're praying for us all. Any more instructions before you depart?

'Yes. You can make up the fires.'

'I'll take care of that,' said Patrick. 'Sam, why don't you and Zoe go to Mass with Emma. Keep her company.'

Sam sat down next to Zoe. 'What, and leave you on your own on Christmas morning? No way.'

'I'm fine on my own,' said Patrick. 'Go on. Go to church with your sister.'

'I'll go, Emma,' said Zoe, jumping enthusiastically to her feet. 'So long as you show me what to do. I've never been in a church.'

'Well, you'll have to hurry,' said Emma. 'I'm leaving in five minutes.'

'I won't be a jiffy. I'll just put my face on. I can have a shower when we get back.'

As Zoe hurried upstairs, Emma looked at her watch.

'Don't worry,' said Sam. 'In five minutes you won't recognise her.' He poured cornflakes into his bowl. 'But it's Father Nick you really want to see, isn't it?'

She gave him a blank look. 'I don't know what you mean.'

'Yes, you do. You want to restore good relations, now Mum's no longer around to exercise her veto.'

'Well, isn't that what we all want?'

'Well said, Emma,' said Patrick, putting his arm round his daughter. 'Time to make a fresh start.'

'Actually, Dad, I was thinking of inviting him round for a drink this evening,'

Patrick hesitated. 'Yes. I suppose you could do that.'

'You don't sound very enthusiastic.'

'Well, he was more your mother's friend really. But invite him, by all means.'

'So, you don't mind?'

Patrick shrugged and smiled. 'Not at all. The more the merrier.'

Chapter Two

Emma walked briskly, making no allowance for Zoe's shorter legs and unsuitable shoes. She felt nervous, but also excited at the prospect of seeing Nick again for the first time since the funeral.

'It's lovely coming here for Christmas,' said Zoe, clattering along beside her. 'I was going to my Mum's, but then Sam said he was spending Christmas with his Dad and would I like to come too. I wasn't sure at first. I mean, it isn't as if we've been going out that long. But I'm really glad I came, because you were all so nice to me last night and not at all like I was expecting.'

'Really,' said Emma, surprised that Zoe could even remember last night. 'And does your Mum live near you?'

'She did. But she's moved now to Chelmsley Wood, so I don't get to see her that much, although it's better now Sam has a car. I don't drive myself, but I'm going to have lessons in the new year when I've saved enough money.'

'Good. So you will be able to see more of her.'

'Yes. I'm an only child, you see, so my Mum's more like my best friend really, even though she's nearly forty, though you wouldn't know it to look at her. We even used to go clubbing together until she met Derek. But we still go to Karaoke together on Thursday nights. Do you like Karaoke, Emma?'

'I can't say I've tried it,' replied Emma evenly as they turned on to the High Street.

'Oh, you'd love it. Mum and me go every Thursday, except when she's on the late shift. Sam doesn't come though, because he thinks he can't sing. But I've told him everyone can sing, if they'd only give it a try. I know he'd like it if he came.'

As the church came into view Emma could feel her heart pounding. Sam was right about her wanting to re-establish good relations with Nick. Apart from a brief conversation at the funeral she hadn't seen or spoken to him in more than two years.

'Yes, my Mum and Dad split up when I was little,' continued Zoe. 'I used to see him quite a lot when he lived near, but then he got married again and moved to Redditch. He's got two children now by his new wife, so I don't suppose he has much time to think about me. But Derek's nice. And his mum's nice too. I call her Nan because I used to call my Dad's mum Gran...'

As Zoe prattled on, Emma found herself thinking of the last time she took this half mile walk through the village to the church. It was last September, three months after her mother's funeral. She had driven over to spend the day with Dad and he suggested they take a walk to the church to inspect the newly erected headstone. He was light-hearted and conversational as they strolled along the high street and she resolved to keep her emotions under control. But, as they arrived at the church, she found herself in tears and soon he was crying too. She was determined not to let it happen today, particularly now Zoe had come with her.

She felt the familiar rush of blood to her face as they entered the churchyard and joined the long queue waiting to greet Father Nick at the door of the church. Yes, she would invite him for drinks this evening. After all, 'the big fall out' as it had come to be known, was with Mum, not the rest of the family. It happened eighteen months ago, shortly before her cancer was diagnosed. Suddenly, in the space of a single weekend, she abandoned the Roman Catholicism into which she had been born and fell out so badly with Father Nick that she refused to see him from that day forward, even on her death bed.

She and Jim were living in Los Angeles at the time and she well remembered her shock at hearing the news. It was the weekend of her Dad's 59th birthday and she telephoned home on the Saturday evening to catch him on Sunday morning before he left for golf. After wishing him a happy birthday, she asked to speak to her mother if she hadn't already left for church. No, he replied, she hadn't left for church and nor would she be going. There had been a bitter exchange between her and Nick. She didn't want to talk about it, but the long and the short of it was that she had abandoned Roman Catholicism for good and her friendship with Nick was also at an end.

Emma asked to speak to her mother, but she was in such an emotional state when she came to the phone, that she decided not to pursue the matter. A few days later came a letter explaining her decision. Her abandonment of the Church might have seemed precipitous, her mother said, but the truth was that she was becoming increasingly disillusioned by all the scandals that seemed to come one after another. In the end, though, it was her disgust at the widespread cover up of the paedophilia scandal that led to her decision. As for Father Nick, she had come to realise that he was a man completely lacking in integrity. She wouldn't go into the details but, as far as she was concerned, she had no wish to see him again or hear his name mentioned.

Emma telephoned her immediately. What had brought this on so suddenly, she demanded? She had held strong views about corruption within the Church for as long as she could remember. So, why now? As for the paedophilia scandal, that too had been going on for years, together with the cover up, but it hadn't undermined her faith until now. More to the point, what had Nick got to do with any of this? If she wanted to abandon her faith that was her affair, but Nick wasn't just her friend, he was a friend of the whole family.

Her mother remained tight lipped. It was a matter of conscience, she said and she didn't want to discuss it further. While she was leaving the Church of Rome, her Christian faith was unshaken, though she had no wish to join any other denomination. As for Nick Hennessy, she wasn't saying the rest of the family shouldn't continue the friendship if they wanted to. But she would prefer it if they didn't invite him to the house as she had no wish to see him. Still she gave no reason for the fallout. Only that she had learned a few things about Father Hennessy that undermined the trust she had placed in him and, as far as she was concerned, she could no longer call him a friend.

She asked her father if he knew why she had taken so much against Nick, but he claimed to be as mystified as everybody else. He could only conclude, he said, that Nick had tried to defend the Church against her many accusations and this had cost him her trust and friendship. Sam was his usual flippant self. If you're that keen to know, why don't you ask Nick, he said? But be careful what you wish for. You might learn a few things you didn't really want to know.

Two months later came the news that something might be amiss with her mother's health. There followed a series of tests, but it wasn't until mid October 2015 that the diagnosis was confirmed. She was suffering from ovarian cancer and the tumour had spread. Emma flew home at once from Los Angeles, renting a house nearby so she could visit her mother every day. Jim followed two months later, having managed to negotiate a transfer to the London office. It was a relatively short illness which her mother bore with great stoicism.

'But then she died, quite suddenly,' continued Zoe. 'They think it was a stroke, so it was a relief in a way, though I was still very upset. I suppose it was the shock....' She stopped in mid sentence and looked apprehensively at Emma.

'I'm sorry?' said Emma composing her face into an expression of sympathetic enquiry. 'Who was this again?'

'My Gran,' said Zoe softly. 'Oh dear. Here am I going on about her dying and you've only recently lost your Mum.'

'That's perfectly all right. She had been ill for some time.'

'Yes, but she wasn't old, was she? I mean not really old like Gran.'

'No. She was fifty six. She died a few days before her fifty seventh birthday.'

As they reached the front of the queue Nick's face lit up immediately. 'Emma! How nice to see you. I was only wondering this morning whether you might be coming home for Christmas.'

'Yes, only a short visit I'm afraid.'

'I was so sorry about your mother, Emma. I telephoned several times in the weeks before she died in the hope she might see me. But it wasn't to be. How is your dad coping?'

'He's fine. Jim and I are here for Christmas and so is Sam. This is Zoe, by the way, Sam's girlfriend.'

Nick put out a firm hand. 'Very nice to meet you, Zoe. Am I right in thinking that Sam is still in bed on this bright Christmas morning?'

'No, he's up,' said Zoe, blushing. 'He's helping Mr Meyer to make the fires.'

'Then you're obviously a good influence on him.' He turned back to Emma. 'Are you here for long?'

'Only today and tomorrow. Jim has to fly to Los Angeles on Tuesday.' Conscious that there were still people queuing behind them, Emma moved into the porch. 'Perhaps I'll see you after Mass. I'm going to visit Mum's grave.' With that she turned and led Zoe into the church.

Chapter Three

Ushering Zoe into a pew towards the back of the church Emma knelt for the briefest of prayers, then sat down and looked around her. In front was a young couple with a baby aged about six months. Leaning over her father's shoulder she stared intently at Emma.

'He's lovely, isn't he,' whispered Zoe.

Emma gave the baby a smile. 'Yes. Though judging by the dress I think it's a she?'

'I mean the vicar. Do you always call him by his first name?'

'Nick? Oh, yes. We've known him since I was a teenager.'

'Sam says your Dad's not a Catholic. And Sam isn't any more. Did you know that?'

'Of course. But our mother was, and we were both brought up as Catholics.'

'Would Nick mind about Sam not being religious any more?'

'I'm sure he wouldn't.'

Zoe was silent for a moment. 'He's good looking, don't you think? For his age, I mean.'

'I suppose he is. I don't think of him in that way.' Conscious that the old lady next to them could overhear, Emma put her finger to her lips.

'Is it true Catholic priests can't marry?' continued Zoe, barely lowering her voice.

'Yes. Catholic priests can't marry.'

'A bit of a waste, don't you think?'

Fortunately at this moment the vestry door opened and two altar boys appeared, one bearing the processional cross, the other a lighted candle. They were followed by Nick, clad now in rich purple robes and swinging incense. The congregation rose in unison as the small procession made its way up the side aisle towards the back of the church, then down the centre aisle to the altar.

As they stood and took up their carol sheets to sing 'Once in royal David's city' Jim appeared suddenly in the centre aisle, looking wildly around him. Seeing them at last he stumbled clumsily past the elderly lady to join them. Ignoring his arrival Emma continued to stare studiously ahead as Nick ascended the steps to the altar. Zoe was right. It was a terrible waste. Nick should never have become a priest.

She was sixteen when he arrived in the parish and she developed an immediate crush on the diffident young priest. Her mother seemed taken with him too, which was surprising as she had never before shown much interest in men. But, as the months went by and he became a regular visitor to the house, the friendship blossomed. Unlike Dad, who had little interest in literature or music, Nick was keenly interested in the arts in all its forms and Emma noticed how her mother became more and more animated as they discussed books they had both read or the music they enjoyed listening to. On these occasions Emma would sit at the table watching jealously as they talked, longing for the moment when he would turn his attention to her to ask what she was reading or what films she had seen.

Her teenage infatuation didn't end when she went to university. Shy like her mother and lacking in confidence, she had only two short lived relationships in all the time she was at Oxford. Meanwhile, with little in the way of a social life to distract her, her obsession with the handsome young priest deepened. Night after night in the solitude of her room, she would fantasise about Father Nick, or Nick, as she preferred to think of him. She would imagine calling on him at his house on some pretext and, once inside, seducing him into breaking his vow of celibacy. Then she would make love to him with such intensity and tenderness that he would be persuaded to give up his vocation to become her lover and eventually, her husband.

Conscious that she was allowing her mind to wander, Emma checked herself. She could never have married Nick, so there was no point in thinking about it. Even if, fifteen years ago, she had found the courage to declare her passion, did she really believe he would have given up his vocation for her sake? Of course not. For better or worse, she was married to Jim, and boring as he could be sometimes, he was a good and loyal husband.

They had been on the same degree course at Oxford, though she couldn't remember speaking to him once during the three years she was there. With his thick horn rimmed glasses and long straggly hair that covered half his face, he was widely regarded as a bit of a nerd. But, six years later, when she came across again him at a business conference in London he was so changed that, at first, she didn't recognise him. He wore the same thick rimmed glasses, but his hair, or what was left of it, was now cropped short and he was wearing a smart business suit.

Over the next few months they met frequently after work and she was soon aware that he had few interests beyond computer technology. But he was attentive to her in an old fashioned way, frequently bringing her flowers when he called to take her out and, as time went by, she got used to his idiosyncrasies and found herself liking him more. She introduced him to classical music, took him to museums and art galleries and sought out plays he might enjoy in the West End or at the National Theatre. Although she could never be sure that he enjoyed these outings as much as she did, he was always happy to go along with whatever she arranged. When, after four years of courtship he plucked up the courage to ask her to marry him, she accepted without hesitation. She wasn't in love with him, but he was an agreeable companion and she knew that, at thirty one, she was unlikely to get a better offer.

As a member of the congregation stepped forward to read the epistle Emma moved closer to Zoe and whispered, 'I hope this isn't too boring for you.

Zoe smiled back sweetly. 'No, I like it. What's happening now?'

'Just a couple of short readings and then it's the sermon. As it's Christmas, Nick will probably just give a little talk to the children.'

As the elderly member of the congregation began to read, the baby in the pew in front began to cry. At first it was little more than an intermittent whimper, but soon the crying became louder and more sustained. Her parents did their best to settle her, but to no avail. Meanwhile the old man reading the epistle continued doggedly on, but before long his voice was drowned and heads were turning increasingly to the source of the commotion. After a few more seconds the mother could stand it no longer. Gathering the baby to her, she squeezed her way along the pew and hurried up the aisle to the exit.

It was all Emma could do not to follow. I'll take care of her, she wanted to call out. Let me look after her and I'll bring her back when she's settled. An absurd thought, of course. What mother would hand her child to a complete stranger, even on church premises? More than once Jim had suggested they go for an IVF consultation and she had to admit that she had been tempted. After all, they had gone in for contraception in the early years (a decision she now bitterly regretted) so where was the problem? But, as Mum had said to her many times, when it comes to faith, you can't cherry pick. You are either a Catholic, or you're not. There are no half measures.

Kissing the bible Nick lifted his head and with a smile wished the congregation a very happy Christmas. As he scanned the aisles, for a moment his eyes seemed to settle on Emma and she felt herself blushing. Then he invited the children to gather round the crib and, in response to his gentle entreaties, soon even the shyest ones left the safety of their parents to creep tentatively forward and join the group. Zoe was right. Nick should never have become a priest.

'Look not on our sins, but on the faith of your Church, and grant us the peace and unity of your kingdom where you live, for ever and ever. The peace of the Lord be always with you'

Emma leaned towards Zoe. 'This is where you greet the people around you. You can wish them a happy Christmas.'

Zoe's eyes lit up. 'Then I'll start with you. Happy Christmas.' Rising on tiptoe, she kissed her on the lips.

Surprised and embarrassed, Emma mumbled her response before turning and offering the briefest of handshakes to the four or five members of the congregation within close range. Meanwhile, Zoe was engaging everyone within reach in friendly conversation and even stepping out to greet people in the aisle.

'Do you want to come to communion?' Emma whispered as Zoe returned to her seat.

'Communion? I don't know. What do I have to do?'

'Come with me. Just keep your head lowered when Nick approaches and he will give you a blessing.'

Emma and Zoe joined the procession to the altar. They were directly behind the young mother who had returned with her baby now sleeping peacefully in her arms. Stepping up to the altar rail she and Zoe knelt and waited as Nick approached with the chalice to deliver the small white wafer to the communicants.

'...the body and blood of Christ….the body and blood of Christ.... the body and blood of Christ....'

Emma raised her head as Nick stood over her.

'...the body and blood of Christ...Emma.'

'Amen.' Lifting her eyes as he placed the wafer in the palm of her hand, she met his gaze. He had added her name. He hadn't needed to, but he did. For that brief moment she was no longer a married woman approaching middle age. She was a blushing teenager again.

Chapter Four

Sending Zoe home with Jim, Emma walked back through the churchyard towards her mother's grave. Tears filled her eyes as she remembered Christmas a year ago when Mum was still eating well and even getting up for short periods. Then her condition began to deteriorate until, by Easter, she was bedridden and unable to keep down her food. For several weeks she remained at home, becoming thinner and more wasted with each day that passed until, in June, it was decided to move her to a hospice. There she lingered for another two weeks, gravely ill but lucid to the end.

Arriving at the grave, she read the engraving on the shiny new granite headstone.

Elizabeth Meyer
Devoted wife and mother
Died 16th July 2016
Aged 56 years

It had occurred to her to ask whether a photograph could have been incorporated into the headstone, like they do on the continent. None of the other graves had photographs, so maybe they weren't allowed in the UK, but she wished she had thought to ask. She could still do so, of course, and maybe she would. She read the four lines again. Succinct and to the point, just as Mum would have wished to commemorate her passing. Because that was how she was – modest, quiet and self effacing, unlike Dad, who could fill a room with his extrovert personality. Her extreme shyness was a pity in some ways because she was a highly intelligent woman and could, almost certainly, have enjoyed a successful career in academia, had she completed her degree course. Raised on the family farm in Donegal, and educated by nuns until she was eighteen, it wasn't until she arrived at Dublin University that she had much contact with the outside world. By which time her modest, deeply religious disposition was so firmly established that Emma often wondered how she and Dad, an agnostic if not an atheist, got together in the first place.

But get together they did, just as he was completing his engineering course and she was coming to the end of her first year studying for a degree in English Literature. Then, during the summer holiday, she developed glandular fever followed by some kind of nervous breakdown, with the result that she never went back to university or, for that matter, back to the family farm in Wexford. Instead, she left Ireland for England where she lodged briefly with Dad's parents until, soon after, they were married.

'Yes, it's a fine headstone, Emma. I think your mother would have approved.'

Emma turned to see Nick coming along the gravel path towards her. In place of his priestly robes he now wore jeans and a polo neck jumper under his coat.

'Hi. I was hoping you would come.' She could feel her heart thumping as he came and stood beside her. 'I'm sorry not to have been in touch. I've been meaning to, but....'

He touched her arm. 'There's no need to explain. I understand.'

'Yes, but it's six months now since the funeral. I should have called on you sooner.'

Nick bent down to remove a dandelion from the grave. 'I've seen your Dad a couple of times. He seems to be managing quite well. How does he seem to you?'

'Okay, I think. I was a bit worried about him in the early days, but he's been better recently. He spends a lot of time at the golf club. I'm not sure what he would do without his golf.'

'I was grateful to him for asking me to take the funeral service. It was comforting to know the entire family hadn't turned against me.'

'Of course we hadn't. We all of us wanted you to take the service, Nick. Not just Dad. Sam and me too. We were only sorry that you and Mum were never reconciled.'

'I'm sorry too. I was very fond of your mother.'

For several seconds Emma was silent. Would he tell her the truth if she asked him? She had worked through several theories over the past eighteen months, but always it was the same one she came back to. Either Nick had made some kind of sexual overture at Mum or, God forbid, it was the other way round.

'What happened, Nick?' she said at last. 'I know Mum had some issues with the Church, but I can't see why they should affect her relationship with you.'

'Yes, I know it seems odd, but it happens sometimes, I assure you. When your mother abandoned the Church, she abandoned me as its representative. You could say I was just part of the collateral damage.'

'But she was so fond of you. Not just as our parish priest. You were her friend, probably her closest friend.'

Nick shook his head. 'I know. And I wish I had a better answer than the one I've given you.'

'She said she no longer trusted you. She said you were a fraud and a hypocrite.'

'She said that, did she? Well, maybe she was right. I mean, the Church has had a lot to answer for in recent times. Pope Pius 12th's failure to speak out against the Holocaust. That's a hard one to explain away. Or the involvement of Catholic priests and nuns in the Rwanda massacre. Then we've had the paedophile scandal, together with the cover up. I know we are talking about people here rather than the institution of the Church but, in the end, I guess it was too much for your mother. The Church was rotten through and through, she said, riddled with corruption all the way up to the top. She said she couldn't stomach it any more.'

'So, she wanted you to abandon the Church too. Was that why she turned against you?'

'That was her position, yes. She said she couldn't understand how I could continue to be a priest within such a corrupt organisation. She said I should give up my vocation.'

'What did you say?'

'I said I couldn't do it. I said that, in spite of everything I couldn't relinquish my vows. After all, there is evil everywhere, in every institution, not just in the Church. I said that I believed my role was to stay and fight corruption from within.'

'And that's why you lost her friendship?'

'Yes. She was angry with me. Perhaps rightly.'

Turning away Emma walked a few steps from the grave. She didn't believe him. Would Mum have ended a friendship of twenty years, simply because he didn't choose to follow her example? No, there had to be something more.

'You said that Jim is flying to the States on Tuesday,' said Nick, following her along the path.

'Yes. The company is going through a reorganisation. There's a chance the European office may be closed down.'

'You mean he might be out of a job?'

'Or we might have to go back to the States.'

'How would you feel about that?'

'I'd prefer to stay in the UK.'

'Then let's hope the meetings go well. I'd be sorry to lose you a second time.' He paused, as if he was about to say more, before deciding against it. 'Well, I'd better let you get back to the family.'

'It was good to see you today, Nick. I'm sorry if you found my questions intrusive'

'Not at all. Though I don't think I've been very helpful. Will you be calling on your dad again soon?'

'Yes, I come over quite often, though usually on weekdays.'

'Then, maybe you could call by one time when you're visiting. I miss those conversations we used to have.'

'I will, I promise.' Emma hesitated. Should she invite him for drinks this evening? Sam seemed okay about it but Dad didn't seem very enthusiastic. Maybe not. She put out her hand. 'Well, goodbye Nick. I'll see you again soon, I hope.'

Chapter Five

'Okay everyone. I think it's time for some champagne.' Patrick Meyer stood with his back to the fire amid the detritus of Christmas wrapping paper.

'I'll get it,' said Sam, putting aside the book of Su Doku puzzles Zoe had given him, in addition to a vulgar, oversized digital watch. 'Come on, Zoe. You can give me a hand.'

As Sam and Zoe disappeared into the kitchen Emma gathered her presents into a neat pile. From Dad, a pair of leather gloves, the wrong size but exchangeable. From Sam and Zoe a frightful necklace that would certainly end up at the charity shop. From Jim, a coffee making machine presumably intended for his own use since he knew perfectly well that she preferred instant. Her own present to her father, a silver framed photograph of her parents taken in happier times, now rested on top of the bookcase.

'Here we are folks,' said Sam appearing from the kitchen with the champagne and glasses, followed by Zoe, tottering on a pair of precariously high heeled shoes and bearing a plate of smoked salmon blinis.

'Zoe wants orange juice,' said Sam, removing the champagne cork. 'Do we have another carton?'

Zoe gave an embarrassed giggle. 'Sorry guys. I thought I should take it easy this morning.'

'There's one in the fridge in the utility room,' said Emma, sitting primly at one end of the sofa and deliberately ignoring Jim at the other end. 'And there are more in the cupboard under the stairs.' She looked at her father, still standing in front of the fire, smiling vacantly. His buoyant mood had dropped since the opening of the presents and she sensed she was the cause. She had been in two minds about giving him the framed photograph and wished now she had saved it for his birthday. He was clearly moved when he opened the box and it troubled her that she might have undermined his resolve to stay cheerful while the family was all together.

The last eighteen months had taken their toll. So much so that for a couple of months after the funeral, she had been seriously worried about him. She would often arrive around midday to find him still in his dressing gown, watching television. Thankfully his depression was short lived. The week following her visit to inspect the headstone she was pleased to find him back to his old self, well groomed, smartly dressed and as cheerful as she had seen him in years. The house too was clean and tidy - so well ordered in fact that she thought he must have taken on a cleaner. This he denied, but the improvement was sustained. Yesterday she and Jim arrived to find everything just as it would have been when Mum was alive - fresh towels folded neatly on the beds, the kitchen and bathrooms clean and tidy and a welcoming fire in the sitting room. There was even a tastefully decorated Christmas tree standing in the corner.

'Well, cheers everybody and a very happy Christmas.' Patrick raised his glass to signal for everyone to chink their own glasses. 'Now, if you will bear with me I thought I would say a few words.'

'Well, keep it short, Dad,' said Sam, putting an arm round Zoe. 'We were thinking of popping down to the pub before lunch.'

'Don't worry, this won't take long.' Patrick paused briefly as he surveyed his family. 'I just want to thank you all for making the effort to be with me this Christmas. It means a lot to me and I appreciate it. I'm just sorry you can't stay longer. Thank you too for your presents and all the champagne and wine you've brought with you. Most generous. And a special welcome to you. Zoe. It's lovely to have you with us.' He paused and looked down. 'Now I know this is going to be a strange Christmas without your mother here to share it with us. But I hope we can still make it a happy occasion.' He looked directly at Emma. 'As I said after the funeral, we mustn't allow our grieving to continue indefinitely, because she wouldn't have wanted it. I know this because she told me so herself. In fact she made me promise that I wouldn't just sit around and mope after she'd gone. And that goes for all of us. So, I want to say to both my children, but to you especially, Emma, I don't want you to worry about me. I appreciate all your visits and phone calls, but I just want you to know that I am managing perfectly well. I have lots of things to occupy me and many friends. Old friends and some new ones too who have been wonderful the way they have all rallied round.'

'New friends, Dad?' said Sam, fetching the second bottle of champagne from the sideboard. 'Are you telling us you've been branching out socially since we saw you last.'

'Well, yes. I suppose I have a bit.' Patrick smiled sheepishly.

'So, who are they, these new friends?' said Sam, refilling his glass. 'More old codgers from the golf club?'

'No, not old codgers and not all male actually.' Patrick glanced at Emma. 'I hope I'm allowed to have friends of the opposite sex now I've turned sixty? Or is that improper, even at my advanced age?'

Sam grinned at him mischievously. 'Is this your roundabout way of telling us you're seeing someone?'

'Ignore him, Dad,' said Emma, glaring at Sam.

Patrick took a long sip of champagne. 'Seeing someone. You know, that's an expression we used when I was young. I didn't realise it was still current. Well, the answer is no, at least not in the sense I think you mean. I'm just saying that I've made one or two new friends recently including, yes, a very nice lady.'

There was a momentary silence.

'Well I think that's lovely,' said Zoe. 'Isn't it Sam?' She pummelled him fondly. 'Don't look at me like that. Why shouldn't your dad have a friend who's a lady?'

Sam shrugged. 'No reason at all. Good on you, Dad. Go for it.'

'Would anyone like some more smoked salmon?' said Emma rising from the sofa. 'We're not having lunch until after three and there's plenty left.'

'Not for me,' said Sam. He looked across at Jim. 'Though Jim looks as if he could use some more, couldn't you Jim?'

'I wouldn't mind,' said Jim, sitting up abruptly. 'Though don't do it just for me.'

Emma got up and walked through to the kitchen. Opening the fridge she took out the second plate of smoked salmon she had prepared on returning from church and removed the cling film. The conversation was continuing in the sitting room and she paused just inside the door to listen.

'So what's her name, this new lady friend of yours?'

Emma sighed. Why was Sam goading him like this?
'She's called Sarah.'
'How old?'
'Oh, I don't know…. forty eight, forty nine.'
She withdrew a little. She didn't want to hear this.
'Married?'
'Divorced actually.'
'Children?'
'Two sons. One in London, one in California.'

Emma walked briskly back into the room. 'I think that's enough interrogation for one day, Sam. Now, who would like some more smoked salmon?'

Deliberately she took her time offering the plate round, hoping a fresh topic of conversation would emerge.

'Does that mean she's on her own for Christmas?' said Zoe, holding an empty glass out to Sam who was following Emma round with the champagne.

'She is actually,' said Patrick. 'Although I think she's going to some friends tomorrow.'

Zoe let out a sigh. 'Oh, I think that's really sad, don't you Emma?'

Emma raised an eyebrow but remained silent

'Why don't you invite her over, Dad?' said Sam. 'There's plenty of food. Why not invite her for Christmas lunch?'

Patrick shook his head. 'No Sam, it's a generous thought but I couldn't do that. This is a family event. I'll give her a ring later to wish her a happy Christmas.'

'Then, invite her for a drink this evening.' Sam looked at Emma. 'Why not? Emma's invited Father Nick.'

'I haven't, actually.' said Emma.

'Why not?'

Emma glowered at Sam, but didn't answer.

'Well, I suppose I could invite her just for a drink,' said Patrick. 'That is, if no one minds. I mean, it would be nice for her to meet you all. And it's not as if we are all together that often.'

'Yes, do it Dad,' said Sam. 'Around 7.00pm. We should have cleared the Christmas dinner by then.'

Patrick looked apprehensively at Emma. 'Only if you're absolutely sure.'

Emma gave a small nod.

'Well, if none of you mind. Yes, I'll give her a ring. No time like the present.'

As Patrick hurried off to his study, Emma stared at her brother in disbelief. Suddenly she felt she could take it no more. Grabbing the silver photo frame from the top of the bookcase she strode out of the sitting room and upstairs to her bedroom, clutching it to her breast. This was no casual friendship. She could tell by his eagerness as he went out to make the phone call. No wonder he was entreating them all not to mourn too long. Because it would hardly do now he had a new woman on his arm and most probably sharing his bed. Sam didn't care, of course. But then, they were two of a kind, Dad and Sam. The same easy charm, the same roving eye. No wonder Sam's marriage didn't last, even if Dad's did.

With tears in her eyes she studied the framed photo. It was taken on holiday about ten years ago. Dad looked much as he did now, though not as grey. Mum, slim and pretty in a blue, sleeveless summer dress stood beside him smiling happily at the camera. Was he faithful? Dad was essentially a man's man, good at sport in his younger days and a passionate follower of it ever since. But he had an eye for women too and they responded to his manly looks and easy charm. She still remembered those parties in Rugby when they were children, watching him through the banisters flirting with the women while their husbands were gathered in the kitchen drinking beer. Then they moved south to Buckinghamshire and his career took off. As Group Sales Director he was often away for two or three weeks at a time, but without the evidence to fuel any suspicion of infidelity, she stopped worrying about him.

There was a knock on the door.

'Emma?'

'Yes?'

She continued gazing out of the window as her father entered the room and came up behind her to rest his hand on her shoulder.

'You're upset?'

'Shouldn't I be?'

'It isn't what you think, Emma. Really it isn't.'

Emma put the photo frame down on the window sill. 'I shouldn't have given you this. It was stupid.'

Now he rested both hands on her shoulders and turned her gently towards him. 'Emma, it was a lovely present. Look, I'm sorry. I'll phone Sarah now and tell her it's not such a good idea after all.'

She shook her head. 'No Dad. You don't have to do that.'

'I do. She'll understand. She'd already said it probably wasn't a good idea.'

Emma raised her eyes to look at him. 'You mean you've already talked of inviting her?'

'No…no, not at all. I just said in passing that you were all here for Christmas and that she might like to pop over sometime.'

Releasing herself Emma moved past him to sit on the bed. 'When did you meet her?'

'It was in October, I think. I've only known her a short time.'

'At the golf club, I suppose.'

He nodded. 'She came in asking for information about membership. She'd just moved into the area and bought a cottage down the road in Saunderton. You'll like her, I'm sure.'

Emma looked away. 'I was going to give you the photo on your birthday. I wish now I'd waited.'

He sat down next to her on the bed. 'Emma it's a lovely present. Look I'm sorry. I wasn't going to mention Sarah at all, but you know what Sam is like. Not that there's anything to hide. She's just a friend, that's all.'

'She knows all about Mum then.'

'Of course. In fact she's the only person I have been able to talk to properly. My golfing pals don't want to be burdened with all my miseries. And Sarah is a good listener.' He was silent for a moment. 'I've been through some dark times Em, as I'm sure you have.'

Emma took a tissue from her sleeve. 'I'm sorry. I overreacted, as usual. No, I'd like to meet her. Really, I would. What time did you invite her for?'

'I said come at seven. I doubt if she'll stay more than an hour.'

She looked up at him and smiled. 'Good. It will be nice to meet her.'

Her father gave her a cautious look. 'Are you sure? It really doesn't matter if you'd prefer me to cancel.'

'No, really. You go down. I'll come down in a minute.'

Chapter Six

As the clock struck seven the family began to assemble to await the arrival of Patrick's new friend, Sarah. All except Emma who remained in the kitchen, dealing with the remnants of Christmas dinner and then busying herself preparing plates of olives and peanuts in readiness for the drinks party. Christmas dinner had gone well. She had taken care to produce the meal exactly as her mother would have done, together with all the trimmings and everyone complimented her on her efforts. Dad was back to his usual jovial self, following this morning's upset, while Sam and Zoe had partially redeemed themselves for last night by helping with the clearing up. She was glad she hadn't invited Nick to the drinks party. Her father's unexpected announcement had changed everything.

'Why are you hiding out here?' said Sam, strolling into the kitchen. 'Worried about meeting Sarah, I suppose.'

'Not especially,' replied Emma. 'So, it doesn't bother you that Dad has a lady friend already.'

'Not at all. And I don't see why it should bother you. You have to let people get on with their lives, Em. Okay, Dad had a good life with Mum, but that marriage is over, and he might live another twenty years. You don't want him to spend the rest of his life living like a hermit, do you?'

'Of course not. But don't you think he might have given it just a little more time?'

'More time? She's a friend, Em, not his concubine. Come on, relax. Let me pour you a drink.'

'No, Sam, please. I don't want any just now.'

Sam looked at his watch. '7.10pm and still not here. Maybe she's got cold feet?' He grinned. 'Have you been watching Dad? He's like a cat on a hot tin roof.' Sam paused.' Ah, do I hear the doorbell?'

'You go through, Sam. I'll come in a moment.'

'No, Em. Come and meet her now. Can't have you skulking in the kitchen like Cinderella.'

Emma followed Sam into the sitting room as Patrick ushered Sarah in from the hall. Slim and elegant in a navy trouser suit, she was every bit as attractive as she had been expecting. She watched her father as he introduced her to each member of the family. Although light hearted in manner, Emma could tell he was slightly on edge.

'...and last, but not least, my daughter. Emma meet Sarah.'

Sarah put out her hand. 'Hello, Emma. Your father has told me a lot about you.'

Emma smiled. 'Only the good things I hope. It's very nice to meet you. And I'm glad you were able to come this evening.'

'Thank you. I wasn't looking forward to spending the entire Christmas with just the television for company.'

'You have a son in London, I gather.'

'Yes, my elder son, Tom. But he's with the in-laws this year. Simon, my other son, lives in Los Angeles.'

Now Sam joined them. 'One tonic with Angosturas. If it's alcoholic at all, it's only marginal, I assure you.'

Sarah gave him a warm smile. 'Thank you. I'll have to take your word for that.'

'So, you met Dad at the golf club,' said Sam, grinning at his father.

'Yes. I had just joined and your father offered to take me round the course.' Sarah looked nervously at Patrick.

'And now you play together?'

'Only occasionally. Patrick is much the better player, but he's very gracious and doesn't complain when he goes round with me.'

'Nonsense,' said Patrick. 'Sarah's a very good player. She certainly gives me a run for my money sometimes.'

'So, what brought you from Northampton to High Wycombe?' said Sam.

Sarah hesitated. 'I'm not sure. I used to come to the Chilterns for holidays when I was a child. It just seemed a nice place to live. And it's not too far from London where most of my clients work....'

As Sam's insistent questioning continued, Emma quietly excused herself on the pretext of checking the food in the oven. She had to concede that Sarah seemed pleasant enough. From what she had gathered so far, she moved to the area six months ago. Having worked in marketing for most of her career, she decided to take the plunge and set up her own public relations company with an office in High Wycombe.

Sam came sauntering into the kitchen. 'So, what do think, Em?'

'We've hardly spoken, but she seems nice enough.'

'And good looking, don't you think? I'll say that for Dad. He knows how to pick them.'

Emma looked crossly at Sam. 'You were certainly giving her the third degree just now.'

'Well, I'm curious. And so are you, if you're honest.'

After taking the vol au vents from the oven, she gave Sam a pile of napkins. 'Here, you can give these out. I hope you're not neglecting Zoe.'

'Oh, don't worry about Zoe Jim's taking good care of her. I've never seen him so animated.'

Emma had noticed that too. Jim and Zoe had struck up a conversation while awaiting Sarah's arrival. Normally he was at his worst talking to women, stammering over his words and failing to maintain eye contact, but with Zoe he was smiling and animated. She could almost believe he was flirting with her.

She followed Sam into the sitting room. Dad and Sarah were now in quiet conversation on one side of the fireplace, with Jim and Zoe on the other side. Zoe was certainly working her spell. Jim was as lively and cheerful as she had ever seen him.

'Here we are, mushroom vol au vents. I hope they're not too hot.' She held out the plate to Jim and Zoe.

'Oh, these are lovely, Emma,' said Zoe, putting one on her napkin. 'Did you make them yourself?'

'No, they're bought, I'm afraid. I only had to heat them.'

'Jim's been telling me about when you were living in Los Angeles. It sounds wonderful. I'd love to go to America.'

'It's not as nice as it sounds, I assure you.' replied Emma curtly. 'If you want to know, I couldn't get back to England soon enough.'

'Now that's not entirely true, Emma,' said Jim. 'We had good times there and made some good friends.'

'Jim says you might be going back soon,' said Zoe.

'Did he now?' said Emma, frowning at Jim. 'Not if I have anything to do with it, we won't....'

As soon as the plate was empty Emma returned with it to the kitchen and put it in the dishwasher. Where was her glass? She must have left it on one of the coffee tables. This wasn't the Christmas she had been expecting. For a start, Dad was far too jovial. She could hear him laughing even now. Seeing him like this no one would believe that he'd lost his wife just six months ago. Sam was right. He couldn't go on grieving forever. But this was too soon, surely.

Sam came into the kitchen again. 'Come on, Em. Come and join us. What's the matter with you?'

'Nothing...I'll come now.'

'You would have preferred Sarah to have been a little less attractive. Is that it? If Dad had befriended a frump, that would have been okay.'

'Of course not.'

'Then come and join in. It's Christmas, for God's sake.'

Taking a clean glass and filling it, Emma followed Sam back into the sitting room and did her best to be conversational and cheerful. To her relief, at 8.30pm Sarah looked at her watch. 'I really must be going. Thank you everyone. It's been a lovely evening.'

'Good bye, Emma,' said Sarah, coming over to her first and kissing her on both cheeks. 'It has been lovely to meet you.'

'Goodbye,' said Emma. 'And good luck with your new venture.'

As Patrick showed her to the door, Emma began gathering up the empty glasses while Sam wandered through to the other room to switch on the television. There was no denying that Sarah had behaved impeccably from the moment she arrived, handling Sam's intrusive interrogation with composure and Zoe's fawning banalities with relaxed good humour.

'Well I think that was a lovely party, don't you Emma?' said Zoe, coming into the kitchen with two half empty plates of crisps and peanuts. 'Shall I put these back in their bags?'

'Yes, they're over by the microwave.' Emma switched on the tap and let the water run until it was hot. What was it about Zoe that grated on her so much? Was it her Birmingham accent, or her tendency to be delighted with absolutely everything around her? All she knew was that her stomach muscles began to tighten every time she appeared.

'Leave the clearing up to me,' said Patrick, returning from seeing off Sarah. He looked happy and contented.' 'I think that went pretty well, don't you? Thank you everyone for making Sarah so welcome.'

Chapter Seven

Emma drove steadily with one eye on the sat nav. She hadn't visited Saskia since she moved to Basingstoke, so she was relying on it to navigate her to her flat, located somewhere in the outskirts. She was angry with Sam. Predictably he hadn't got round to telephoning Saskia yesterday and it was only because of her constant badgering that he managed it this morning. Unfortunately, by the time he rang, Tommy had gone on an outing with his maternal grandparents. So, she decided to drive over and see Saskia herself and perhaps see her nephew later in the day. She would hardly be missed. Dad, Sam and Zoe were going to a football match, while Jim would certainly be spending the day glued to his laptop and worrying over his presentation.

 She felt guilty that she hadn't been in touch with Saskia since the funeral. Best friends at university, it was she who introduced her to Sam in the first place. He arrived unannounced at her Oxford college one afternoon in her final year looking much in need of a meal. So, having decided to take him to the local pub, she invited Saskia to join them. He then spent the night sleeping in her armchair and the following morning, she sent him back to Birmingham with ten pounds in his pocket for the train fare. Saskia mentioned him only a couple of times over the next few days, so it was a surprise to learn, shortly after their graduation, that they had moved in together and Saskia was pregnant.

 'Emma! So, you found us all right.'

 Saskia came down the path as Emma was fetching flowers from the back seat and the two of them hugged and kissed like the long lost friends that they had become since her divorce from Sam five years before. She appeared to have put on weight since the funeral and it was only as she was leading her into an untidy front room that she realised she was pregnant.

'Well, you're a dark horse,' Emma said with a laugh. 'Are you what I think you are?'

'Yes. Four months, unfortunately,' said Saskia ruefully. 'Something I could do without right now.'

So, you're in a new relationship?'

She shook her head. 'I thought I was, but it seems not.....Tea, coffee? Or would you like something stronger? You're staying for lunch, I hope.'

Over the next hour the two friends caught up on each other's lives. Since the divorce, Saskia appeared to have had a string of relationships while teaching English and History part time at a comprehensive in Birmingham. She had moved to Basingstoke with her latest partner only in June, at which point he promptly got her pregnant before setting off for Hong Kong to take up what he described as a more rewarding position.

'Are you planning to follow him out there?' enquired Emma.

Saskia shrugged. 'It seems less likely by the day.'

But he'll support you, surely. He'll have to.'

'I don't think so. Knowing Ted, he's probably got another woman by now. My fault. I don't seem to be any good at choosing men. How is Sam, by the way? I gather he's got a new girlfriend.'

'Yes, Zoe. A hairdresser, barely out of her teens.'

'He sounded pretty smitten with her when he rang this morning.'

'Oh. He told you about her, did he?'

'He did. He sounded as happy as I've ever known him.'

Saskia and Sam's marriage was, of course, doomed from the start. Sam had his father's easy charm, but he could hardly be described as clever, which Saskia certainly was. He had been a difficult child as far back as Emma could remember and his rebellious behaviour continued to cast a pall over family life until the day he left home. When, at sixteen, he announced that he was going to join the army, neither parent worked very hard at persuading him to change his mind. It might sort him out, said Dad. At least it will teach him some discipline and self control. Mum, who by this time was thoroughly worn out by his disruptive behaviour, made no objection.

'I'm sorry about my brother,' sighed Emma. 'I bet you curse me for ever introducing him to you.'

'Not at all. Sam was a good husband. It was me who wrecked the marriage, not him.'

'Really? What do you mean?'

'I had an affair. Didn't he tell you the whole lurid story?'

'No, he didn't. What happened?'

'It was soon after our honeymoon. I got a job at the university and fell head over heels for my professor. It didn't last, of course. Derek was a family man. I should have realised he wasn't going to leave his wife for me.'

'Did Sam know about this?'

'Oh, yes. I told him. He was upset, of course, but he was very good about it. Told me I'd been a silly girl and not to do it again. But he never quite trusted me after that. Understandably. I'm sorry, Emma. I expect you hate me now. But I thought Sam would have told you everything by now.'

'No. He never mentioned anything about your relationship. I always thought it was Sam who was the philanderer.'

'No, not at all. Sam's not like that. He put up with my wayward behaviour for a lot longer than I deserved.' Saskia smiled. 'You're a lucky girl, Em. You've got a good husband who obviously adores you. Don't make the mistakes I made.'

'You mean Jim?' said Emma. 'If he cares for me at all, he has a funny way of showing it.'

'Well, maybe you don't bring out the best in him.' Saskia laughed. 'Come on, Em, Don't give me that surprised look, You can be pretty intimidating, you know, once you've got the bit between your teeth. Even I was frightened of you when we first met. Still, who am I to give advice? Tell me, how's your Dad?'

'Oh, he's doing quite well,' said Emma, still puzzling over what Saskia had just told her. 'Actually he's got himself a girlfriend already.'

Saskia shrugged. 'Well, I don't blame him. He's had a hard time, especially these last few years.'

'Yes. Nursing Mum through her illness certainly took its toll.'

'Not to mention all that business before. He must have been at his wit's end.'

'You mean her falling out with the Church?.'

'Saskia looked momentarily disconcerted. 'Of course, you and Jim were in America, weren't you.'

'I know Mum fell out badly with Nick Hennessy I still haven't got to the bottom of that. Is that what you're referring to?'

'No. I've probably got it all wrong. It was just a few things I heard from Sam. You should really ask him. Come on. I'm starving, Let's get some lunch. '

Driving back from Basingstoke Emma tried to make sense of everything she had learned on her visit. She had certainly misjudged Saskia whom she had always looked up to as someone endowed with looks as well as brains, yet seemed to have squandered both. She was realistic enough to realise that there were always two sides to a marriage break up, but there was no doubt that the picture Saskia painted of Sam was very different from the feckless individual she had always assumed him to be. Over lunch she had become quite emotional as she talked of the mess she had made of her life since Oxford and how much she wished she could turn the clock back. By the time she had drunk two large glasses of wine she was in full confessional mode, tearfully admitting to having embarked not on one, but on a series of short lived affairs within a year of her marriage to Sam.

And what was she to make of her remark about Dad being at his wits end even before Mum's illness?. Was there more to the fall out with Nick that she hadn't been told? She had tried to draw Saskia out further during lunch but she clearly didn't want to say any more on the subject.

She arrived home to find Dad and Zoe watching television and Sam sprawled across the other sofa fast asleep. As expected Jim was up in the bedroom, still working at his laptop.

'Well,' she said, taking a pair of jeans from the wardrobe. 'You've certainly been great company this Christmas.'

Jim looked up defensively. 'Sorry, but you know how it is. I'll be fine once this crisis is over. How was Saskia?'

'A mess. The house was a tip too, but I was expecting that. She was always pretty chaotic. No it's her personal life that worries me. I thought that once she and Sam got divorced she would be okay. But she isn't. She seems to have had a string of partners since then, all of them useless, The last one got her pregnant before shoving off to Hong Kong without leaving any means of getting in touch. '

'A pity,' said Jim, without looking up.' I liked Saskia. She's a kind person.'

Emma didn't answer. Was that his way of saying that she wasn't a kind person? Maybe Saskia was right. Maybe she didn't bring out the best in him.

'Did you learn anything else?' he said, still tapping away at the keyboard.

She looked at him with contempt. 'Not really. At least nothing that would interest you.'

Chapter Eight

Back home after Christmas, Emma was clearing the breakfast things, while Jim was upstairs finishing his packing. The morning had started bright and sunny with the light scattering of snow gone, apart from a small area in the shade of the hedge.

'Have you seen my reading glasses?' Jim called from the landing.

'There's a pair on the mantelpiece in the sitting room.' Jim and his possessions were easily separated.

'And my silver cuff links...' She heard him coming downstairs and going into the lounge. 'Seen those anywhere?'

'They're in the utility room by the washing machine. You left them in the shirt you wore on Christmas Day.'

'Thanks.'

As Jim passed through the kitchen, Emma sat down at the table and opened her iPad. She typed Sarah Campion into Google. There were several Sarah Campions but she quickly found the website she was looking for. *'Sarah Campion, Public Relations Consultancy, 11 Thurlow Road, High Wycombe.*

'I see Sarah Campion used be marketing manager at Furlow and Steel,' she said, as Jim came back downstairs with his suitcase. 'That name rings a bell.'

'It's a subsidiary of the group your Dad worked for,' said Jim putting on his coat. 'They're based in Northampton.'

'So, that's why I've heard of it. Odd then that he's only just met her.'

'Not really. ATZ is a big group.'

'I know. But Dad was group sales director. If she was the marketing manager of a subsidiary, he must have come across her at some point.'

Jim shrugged. 'I suppose so. Anyway, the taxi will be here any moment. Are you going to see me off the premises?'

'Sorry, yes.' Emma got up and came over to him. 'Have a good trip.' She gave him a perfunctory kiss. 'Good luck with your meetings.'

He held on to her so tightly that she felt mildly disconcerted. This wasn't at all like the Jim she knew.

'I'm sorry to mess up the Christmas break. You know that, don't you.'

'Of course I do.'

He studied her face. 'But you're still cross with me. About last night.'

'It's okay,' she said, pushing him playfully away.' For the third night in a row Jim was fast asleep by the time she came out of the bathroom.

'It's just that I've got a lot on my mind right now. I'll be on better form once I know where I stand.'

'I know.'

'And if all else fails, we can still go for IVF. We've got the money and it's not as if the Pope...'

'Jim,' she said crossly, 'you know my views on IVF'.

'But lots of people do it. Catholics included. You've said that yourself.'

Emma looked away. 'Well, we can talk about it when you get back. Off you go. That sounds like your taxi hooting.'

As the taxi drew away Emma sat down at her iPad and resumed her research. Born in 1967, Sarah Campion attended the local comprehensive school, before going on to read Business Studies at Manchester. Following graduation she spent the next few years in London, working in advertising. There followed a ten year break, presumably to raise her children, before resuming her career in 2008. In 2009 she joined Furlow and Steel as marketing manager, a position she held for six years before leaving to set up her own public relations consultancy.

Emma picked up her phone and tapped in her brother's number.

'Sam Meyer.'

'Hello, Sam.'

'Hi Em. How's things? Has Gentleman Jim departed for the States yet?'

'He left a few minutes ago. Listen, are you by yourself?'

'Yes. Zoe's gone shopping. Why?'

'I've been doing some research on Dad's new lady friend. Did you know she used to work for Furlow and Steel?'

'I've never even heard of Furlow and Steel. What of it?'

'It's part of the group that Dad worked for.'

'So?'

'Well, don't you think it strange? I mean, Dad saying they only met in September. Yet she used to work for the same group as a marketing manager, which is not exactly a junior role, so their paths were bound to have crossed. She left in 2016, about the same time as Dad took early retirement. Now she's moved just down the road from him...'

'Hold it, Em. Where is all this leading?'

'I would have thought that was obvious. Dad was group sales director at the same time as Sarah was the marketing manager of one of the subsidiaries. In which case, he must have known her. So, why didn't he come clean and say so, instead of pretending they'd only just met?'

Sam was silent for a moment. *'I can think of one good reason.'*

'What?'

'You and your suspicious mind. If Dad had announced on Christmas morning that Sarah was a former work colleague, you would have started putting two and two together before the words were even out of his mouth.'

'Of course I wouldn't.'

'If you want my advice, Em, keep your nose out of things that don't concern you. It's Dad's life, not yours.... Now, what are you doing for New Year?'

'I don't know. With Jim away, I'll probably just have an early night.'

'You're very welcome to come and spend it with Zoe and me.'

Emma hesitated. 'Thanks, Sam, but I can't think about that at the moment. Can I get back to you?'

'Okay, but remember what I've just said. Don't meddle!'

Putting down the telephone, Emma gazed at the iPad screen. Was Dad lying about meeting Sarah only last September? Whatever else she was, Sarah Campion was a striking looking woman and Dad always had an eye for attractive members of the opposite sex. No, she was letting her suspicions run away with her. Still, it seemed odd that Sarah should choose to uproot from Northampton to set up her business in High Wycombe of all places, and then come to live in Saunderton, just five miles down the road from Dad.

Closing her iPad she picked up her car keys. Best to have it out straight away. Or it would fester.

Chapter Nine

Emma pulled into the drive of her father's house to find him standing in the porch. As she got out of the car he came towards her.

'Well, this is a nice surprise.'

'Is it?' She kissed him. 'You look as though you were expecting me.'

'I was, in a way. Sam telephoned to say you might pay me a visit. Sarah's here as it happens. Come in.'

As they went indoors Sarah appeared in the hall. 'Hello Emma, how nice to see you again.'

'Hi.' She managed a smile.' No, I won't stay. It was just something I wanted to see Dad about.'

'Then I'll make myself scarce. You two go into the sitting room while I make some coffee.'

As Sarah disappeared into the kitchen, Emma followed her father into the sitting room where they sat down facing one another.

'So, tell me what's troubling you.'

'Didn't Sam tell you?'

'He did, actually. You think I lied about when Sarah and I first met. That's it, isn't it?'

'Well, did you?'

Patrick gave a long sigh. 'Yes, I did and I'm sorry. Sarah and I did know one another in ATZ, though only as colleagues. It's just that I didn't want any of you to get wrong ideas. It was my decision. Sarah was all for coming clean from the outset.'

'I see,' said Emma, wishing now she had taken Sam's advice. 'How well did you know each other?'

'As I say, we were work colleagues, that's all. And our paths didn't cross that much. After all, Sarah was in Northampton and I was in London most of the time.'

As Sarah came in from the kitchen bearing a tray of coffee, Emma determined to put her suspicions to one side. Sam was right. Why shouldn't Dad and Sarah be friends? Dad may have had a roving eye but she doubted he would ever have been unfaithful. In spite of their very different interests and temperaments, he and Mum were devoted to one another. True, there were difficulties in the early years as they tried in their different ways to deal with Sam, but never once did she hear them argue. Nor was there any tension between them in matters of religion. In spite of being a non believer, Dad made no objection to Sam and herself being brought up as Catholics and attending Catholic schools. He even accompanied them to Mass sometimes.

Sarah poured the coffee. 'Patrick tells me you used to work for the BBC, Emma. Do you have any plans to return there?'

'I don't think so. Jim's job is a bit uncertain at the moment, so we may have to move.'

'Not to America, I hope. Jim said it was a possibility, but you weren't keen.'

'As far as I'm concerned it isn't even a possibility. Jim knows my views. We are not going back to America under any circumstances.'

As they talked Emma had to concede that Sarah was a relaxed and friendly communicator, volunteering without prompting that her husband left the family home when their younger boy was two, leaving her a single parent with no job and no means of financial support. Fortunately her parents stepped in with financial assistance and they were able to keep body and soul together. Then she got the job with Furlow and Steel which boosted her income as well as restoring her self confidence.

She was about to probe more deeply into Sarah's time with Furlow and Steel when her father moved the conversation on to Sam and Zoe. Not the partner he would have expected Sam to choose, he said, but a nice girl all the same. And evidently fond of Sam, which was the main thing.

'Yes, I talked to Zoe quite a lot,' said Sarah. 'I thought she was charming. Is she at all like Sam's ex wife?'

Patrick laughed. 'Not a bit. Saskia was what you might call an academic. Very bright girl. She was your best friend at university, wasn't she, Em?'

'She was.'

'Patrick tells me it was you who introduced them,' said Sarah.

'I did.'

'And if it wasn't for Sam's fecklessness, they would be together now,' said Patrick.

In the awkward silence that followed, Emma considered briefly coming to her brother's defence. Instead she stood up. 'I'd better go. Goodbye Dad. Very nice to see you again, Sarah.'

Following her to the door Patrick put his arms around her. 'Good bye, Darling. I hope we've cleared the air.'

'We have,' she said, kissing him. 'I hope you're not cross with me.'

'Not at all. My fault entirely.'

Sarah came forward and clasped her hands. 'Goodbye Emma. I do hope we can become friends.'

'Yes, I'm sure we can.' As their eyes met she wondered whether she would be harbouring these suspicions if Sarah wasn't so attractive? She certainly looked much younger than her forty nine years. It was also perfectly obvious that Dad was besotted with her. She could tell from the way he was looking at her even now.

'Actually, Dad.' she said, turning to him, 'Jim's been complaining about losing one of his silver cuff links. I'll just go upstairs and have a look in the bedroom in case he dropped it there.'

Moving swiftly past them, Emma went upstairs, glancing round as she turned the corner of the landing to make sure she wasn't being followed. Then, walking straight past the room she and Jim occupied over Christmas, she pushed open the door of her father's bedroom. Her Christmas present, the silver framed photograph, was nowhere to be seen. Nor was the small photo of the two of them that he normally kept on his bedside table. Moving to the far side of the bed, she lifted the pillow. Underneath was a nightdress.

'No, they must be at home somewhere,' she said, coming downstairs. 'Jim's always losing things.'

A minute later she was driving home, her cheeks wet with tears.

Chapter Ten

Emma sat at the kitchen table, her iPad open in front of her. She hadn't eaten since her early breakfast with Jim, but she wasn't hungry. How could Dad be sleeping with another woman already, and in the same bed that he and Mum had slept in for nearly forty years? No doubt Sam would say that six months was a long time, but that was Sam. He was never close to Mum, never really close to either of them. She felt a sudden shudder. Maybe the affair began when Dad was still working. Maybe it had been going on for years, even through Mum's illness. After all, Sarah Campion joined Furlow and Steel in 2009, so it was reasonable to assume that Dad would have known her. He might even have recruited her in the first place. And he must have met up with her at least four or five times a year on his regular round of the subsidiary companies, not to mention those long overseas trips he made, accompanied by personnel from one or more of companies in the group. As a marketing manager she must have joined him on at least some of those trips.

Opening her iPad she typed ATZ into Google and went to the group's home page. Clicking on Furlow and Steel she opened each tab in turn looking for any reference to the two of them. Under *News Releases* her father's name came up several times, but not Sarah Campion's. She clicked on *Publications* and skimmed through their marketing magazines for each of the last four years. Here she found what she was looking for.

Emma closed her iPad? She had to talk to someone. There was a time when her first port of call would have been Saskia but, after visiting her on Boxing Day, she wasn't sure she would give her a balanced judgement. She decided to call Sam.

'Hello Sam, it's me.'

Silence.

'Sam, are you there?'

'Em, what did I say to you? Didn't I say keep your nose out? But you don't listen, do you!'

'And you didn't keep my confidence. You warned Dad I was driving over. Why did you do that?'

'Because I knew you weren't going to take my advice. Listen, Em, Dad and Sarah's relationship is their business. Okay?'

'But he's still lying, Sam. He lied over Christmas and he lied again to me today.'

'What do you mean he lied to you again?'

'First he said he and Sarah only met last September. Today he admits they did know each other in ATZ, but their paths rarely crossed.'

'So?'

'I've been doing some research. Sarah Campion travelled all over the world with Dad – Hong Kong, India, Australia. See for yourself. Go to the ATZ home page and click on *Publications* in the Furlow and Steel section.'

'Which you've already done, I assume. So what will I find there? Pictures of the two of them tucked up in bed together?'

'No, but there are several references to her on Dad's overseas trips as well as photographs. Look at the photograph on page six of the 2013 magazine. He is standing right next to her. She was also on that USA trip he did in 2015, just before he retired to look after Mum.'

'I see. So you think they were having an affair, do you? Just because they went on a few business trips together and you've found a photograph where he is standing next to her.'

'No. I'm saying that he must have known her quite well. Even very well. Which is not what he's admitted to so far.'

'Listen, Em. Dad was group sales director. He had whole delegations travelling with him. She was just one of a team. As for the photograph, he had to stand next to somebody.'

'Fine. Okay. You think their relationship was innocent. I don't. Let's leave it there, shall we.'

'Em, for God's sake. Why are you behaving like this? Why are you so judgmental? Everything's okay between you and Jim, isn't it?'

'Of course it is. What has Jim got to do with this? Look, that's not the only thing....'

'Leave it , Em. I'm telling you. If you want to ruin your relationship with Dad, you're going about it in exactly the right way.'

Holding the handset away from her for a moment Emma breathed deeply. 'Okay.' She sighed. 'Forget I phoned you.' She was going to tell him about the nightdress, but what was the point?

'Have you decided about New Year yet? Come on, Em. You need to cool it. Come to Birmingham and celebrate with us. Zoe was very taken with you, by the way. There'll be no big party. Just the three of us.'

Chapter Eleven

Emma switched on the bedside light. 2.45am. If she had slept at all it could only have been for a few minutes. This was stupid. She was letting her imagination run away with her. Okay, Dad was sleeping with Sarah Campion. She didn't like it but, as Sam reminded her, Dad wasn't the kind of person to sit around and mope. And just because Sarah once worked in the same group as Dad, it didn't necessarily mean the relationship began when Mum was still alive. So, why was she even allowing herself to think it? Dad was devoted to Mum. Didn't he give up his job so he could nurse her through her illness? There were times, of course when he went off during the day for a round of golf, or to meet up with ex colleagues, but did she really think that was just an excuse to spend a morning or afternoon in the arms of Sarah Campion?

She was about to switch off the light when the telephone rang.

'Emma? Have I woken you? Sorry, it's Jim.'

'Jim!... Do you realise what time it is?'

'Yes, and I'm really sorry, Em. but I seem to have mislaid the spreadsheet I was working with all through Christmas.'

'What do you mean you've mislaid it? I thought you couldn't lose anything on a computer these days.'

'I know. I thought I had saved it, but I've done a thorough search and it isn't here.'

'So, where is it?'

It must still be on my desktop. I need it, Em. I'm doing my presentation tomorrow and my figures just don't add up.'

Emma got wearily out of bed. 'All right. But you'll have to be patient. I know nothing about your computer. I don't even know how to switch it on.'

'That's fine. Tell me when you're at my desk and I'll give you the password.'

Fifteen minutes later Emma still hadn't located the file Jim was looking for and he was getting increasingly agitated. *'Are you sure you're looking in the right folder? It has to be there.'*

'Jim, I'm looking where you told me to look. I can look in other folders if you want me to. There's one here called *Dead Files.* Maybe you put it in there.'

'No, it's not in there. Maybe it's in the Recycle Bin. I did a tidy up on Sunday. There's just a chance I binned it in error.'

Emma opened the Recycle Bin and scrolled down an endless stream of thumbnail icons, mostly Word and Excel documents, but also some deleted music and, to her surprise, a few picture and video files.

'There's a hell of a lot of stuff here, Jim. I hope you don't expect me to trawl through everything.'

'No. There's no need for that. Go to the little box at the top of the screen with a magnifying glass icon...'

At last they located the relevant file, which Emma emailed to Jim as an attachment. 'Is that it?' she said irritably. 'Do I now have permission to go back to bed?'

'Thank you, Em. You've saved my life. I'm really sorry to have messed up your night.'

'Well, you've certainly managed that. Not that I was really asleep when you rang...' She was about to tell him about her visit to her father, but she could tell he wasn't in a listening mode. 'Anyway, good luck with your presentation. I hope it goes well.'

Putting down the handset Emma stared at Jim's computer screen. What were those picture and video files? Jim never took photographs. He didn't even own a camera. Opening the Recycle Bin a second time she scrolled down until she came to the first JPG file. It was titled *Kim* but the image was too small to make anything out. She double clicked and a new window opened inviting her to restore the file. Restore to where? She read the information more carefully. *Kim. JPG file. Origin: Dead Files*. Clicking on *Restore,* she went to the *Dead Files* folder and clicked on *Kim*. A photograph of a naked young woman filled the screen, sitting astride a motor bike. Closing the file she returned to the Recycle Bin, and ran her mouse over the next three files – *Wild Party, What Samantha Saw, The Orgy Room.* Restoring these to the *Dead Files* folder. she double clicked on *Wild Party*. To her dismay, this wasn't a photograph but a video. In a tawdry domestic setting a dozen or more men and women, all of them naked, were engaged in a variety of sexual acts, mostly in pairs, but some in threesomes.

Emma's hand was shaking so much now that she could barely control the mouse as she closed the file and shut down the computer. She knew this kind of material was freely available on the internet and that there were men who enjoyed looking at it. But not Jim, surely. She had always assumed it appealed only to men on the fringes of society - perverts, drug addicts, paedophiles - not successful, educated, married men like Jim.

At 4.45am Emma slipped into a cold bed. She had gone back to Jim's computer and looked at his search history.

Sure enough, interspersed among normal business searches were several sites containing, to judge by their titles, explicit sexual material. Returning to the Recycle Bin she trawled through to the end, in search of more files of the kind she had found earlier. Finding none, she returned to the *Dead Files* folder and steeled herself to watch *What Samantha Saw* and *The Orgy Room*. These also depicted men and women engaged in every type of sexual act, the men mostly clothed or semi-clothed, the women naked. She watched, horrified but at the same time mesmerised, as the camera swooped in and out on scenes of brazen sex, accompanied by a soundtrack of grunts, moans and laughter. By the time she had watched half of the second video, she could take no more. This was filth, unspeakable filth. Only a sick person could enjoy looking at such material.

She would have to confront him, there was no doubt about that. Unpleasant as it would be, this wasn't something that could be postponed. Not now, perhaps, but as soon as he returned, as soon as she got him home from the airport. Before he had even unpacked his case, she would sit him down, tell him what she had discovered on his computer and demand an explanation. Except there could be no explanation. That material hadn't found its way on to his computer by accident, so there was no point in him pretending that it had.

But what then? Could she continue to be married to him, let alone share her bed with a man who took pleasure in this kind of filth. What options did she have? Separation? Divorce? For all his faults and limitations she and Jim had rubbed along well enough until now. It wasn't the most exciting of marriages, yet the thought of splitting up, selling the house and dividing their assets between them was as bleak as it was daunting. She would be poorer certainly. Not as poor as Saskia, perhaps, but poorer all the same. And lonely too. She was thirty six. The thought of being single again and trying to make a new life for herself was frightening. Saskia seemed to have made a complete mess of her life since she and Sam split up and she could see herself going the same way.

It was with these troubled thoughts running through her head that, just before dawn, Emma finally fell asleep.

Chapter Twelve

For the first few moments on waking Emma could almost believe that the events of the last twenty four hours were nothing more than the dislocated recollections of a nasty dream. But as she got out of bed she knew this was no dream. The pictures and videos on Jim's computer were as real as the nightdress she found under the pillow of her father's bed.

The only person she could think of to talk to was Sam, but she knew already what his response would be. So, Jim looks at pornography. It's what men do. Get over it. As for the nightdress under the pillow, what was she doing snooping in Dad's bedroom anyway?

After a morning of brooding indecision, Emma decided she had to get out of the house. Fetching her walking gear from the garage she threw it into her car and set off. Fifteen minutes later she was walking up the road from Wendover in the direction of the Coombe Hill monument. She would go up via the footpath and back down the bridleway. Not a long walk, but it would help to clear her head.

She walked quickly, staring grimly ahead as she made the long ascent, barely aware of the panorama opening up to her right. Everything was falling into place now - why Jim wasn't interested in having sex, why she had to make the running every time. Normal sex wasn't enough for him any more. It had to be perverted sex, obscene sex, the kind only pornography could provide. Well, if that was what he wanted, he was welcome to it. He could move out as soon as he got back from Los Angeles and take his computer with him.

As she approached the monument Emma picked out the silhouette of a man and a dog standing on the monument steps, looking out over the vale. There was something about the way he stood that looked familiar but she couldn't be sure. As she came nearer he turned in her direction and then she knew. It was Nick Hennessy.

'Hi,' she called out. 'This is a surprise, seeing you.'

With a cheery wave, Nick came down the path to greet her. 'Emma. But I thought you'd gone home. You're not still staying at your Dad's, are you?'

'No. But Amersham's only a fifteen minute drive and I needed some fresh air.'

'Then we've both had the same idea.'

Could she tell Nick her problem and get his advice? Priests were trained in such matters and she could be certain, at least, that he would treat anything she told him as confidential. Except that she didn't want to talk to a priest. Right now it was a friend she needed. Someone who would sympathise and comfort her.

'Will you do me a favour, Nick,' she said, already close to tears. 'Walk with me back down to Wendover. Then I could drive you home.'

Nick gave her a look of concern. 'Yes, of course. So long as you don't mind having a muddy dog in your car.'

As they walked back down the footpath towards the bridleway Emma was already having second thoughts. This was something that centred on the most intimate part of her marriage. Yet here she was, about to confide it to someone she had been half in love with for as long as she had known him. No, she couldn't do it. It would be nothing short of a betrayal.

By the time they reached the bridleway the number of walkers sharing the path had thinned out. Pausing to let the dog rummage in the undergrowth, Nick turned to Emma. 'I can see something's troubling you, Emma. Do you want to talk about it?'

Emma shook her head. 'No, it's nothing. Really. Nothing at all.' She turned away, her eyes stinging with tears.

He put out a tentative hand and touched her arm. 'But you're upset.'

'I know...I'm sorry...' Her words were lost as she broke down in a flood of tears.

Drawing her to him he put his arms around her and for several seconds neither spoke. Then, taking a tissue from her pocket Emma blew her nose and wiped her eyes. 'Let's walk. It's easier if we walk.'

As they made their way down the bridleway, Emma poured out the whole story. How Jim had asked her to go on his computer to look for his lost file, And how, in the course of looking for the file in the Recycle Bin, she came across pornographic photos and videos.

For a while Nick didn't respond. Then he said, 'How do you know they were pornographic? You can't look at files once they have been moved to the Recycle Bin.'

'I know, I followed the instructions on the screen and restored them to their original folder.'

'And you looked at them there?'

'Yes.'

'Have you returned them to the Recycle Bin?'

'I have, actually. But does it matter? I'm going to confront him anyway.'

'I see.' Nick turned to look at her. 'Are you sure you want to do that?'

She stared back in disbelief. 'Yes, Nick, of course I'm sure. I can't go on living with a man who secretly indulges in that kind of filth.'

When Nick didn't answer Emma started to cry. 'I thought you of all people would be on my side. These weren't just pin ups, Nick. They were obscene photos. Videos too. Filthy, disgusting videos. People engaged in all manner of sex acts. I'm not naive. I know some people like looking at this kind of thing, but I would never have believed it of Jim. I mean, why would he want to look at pornographic videos? That's what I don't understand.'

Nick looked at her questioningly. 'But you're happy, the two of you? You sleep together?'

Emma shrugged. 'We sleep in the same bed, if that's what you mean.' She paused. 'You probably don't know this but, for the last five years, we've been trying for a baby. Or I have. Jim never seems to want sex. That can't be normal, can it?'

A silence fell between then as they negotiated the slippery steps down to the gate. On reaching the road, Nick said, 'Did the videos you looked at contain anything really shocking? I mean content that you feel you should report to the police?'

Emma looked at him doubtfully. 'If you mean were there children involved, the answer is no. At least, not in the ones I saw.'

'Did they depict violence, sexual assault, rape – that kind of thing?'

'No. There was plenty of male dominance, but I wouldn't call it violent.' Emma stopped and turned to face him. 'I know you think I'm naive, Nick. But this is filth I'm talking about. Obscene, disgusting filth. People having sex with two or three people at a time. You're not telling me that normal men enjoy looking at this kind of material.'

Nick paused before answering. 'You say that you are anxious to get pregnant, but Jim doesn't seem interested in sex. Have you considered that the two things might be connected? I mean, perhaps he is feeling inadequate, feeling the need for a bit of extra stimulus to bring him up to scratch.'

They continued down the road in silence until they reached the car. Then Emma said, 'Now I don't know what to think.' She managed a smile. 'Jump in and I'll take you home..

Driving Nick back to Princes Risborough, Emma's mind was in such a state of confusion that she was quite unable to turn the conversation to lighter matters and Nick too seemed in no mood to talk. Ten minutes later she pulled up outside his house.

Nick reached into the back seat for his coat. 'Thank you, Emma, that's very kind. Now, can I offer you a cup of tea?'

Emma hesitated. 'No. I'd better get back. I feel I've taken enough of your time already.'

'I'm afraid I haven't been very helpful'

'But you have, Nick, really you have.'

'It's just that I don't want you to judge Jim too harshly. He's a good man.' He smiled. 'Come on. It's not often I get the chance to invite a lady in for tea. And I've even got some cake.'

Chapter Thirteen

As Nick went to the kitchen to make the tea, Emma sat down in one of the two armchairs situated on either side the fireplace. She looked around her. The velour upholstery and heavily brocaded curtains might have been inherited from the previous occupant, but surely not the pictures and ornaments. Yet these too were disappointingly impersonal. The oval mirror above the fireplace told her no more about Nick Hennessy than the three rather faded watercolours on the opposite wall, or the standard lamp with the beige fringed shade in the corner. The only item in the room that might not have come from a house clearance sale was on the mantelpiece - a small silver framed photograph of two young men standing arm in arm and smiling at the camera.

'Here we are,' said Nick, coming in with a tray and setting it down on a wicker stool. 'Milk and sugar?'

'Just milk, thanks,' said Emma. 'This is nice, to be waited on for once.'

'And can I offer you some cake. Tesco's finest, I assure you.'

'Well, just a small slice. I don't normally eat cake.'

'Oh, I think a little indulgence now and again is no bad thing.' He smiled as he met her gaze. 'Anyway, you have nothing to worry about. You're as slim now as the day I first saw you.'

'I hardly think so.'

'Yes, really. You've barely changed at all. At least, not in my eyes.'

Was he flirting with her? No, priests didn't flirt. To Nick she was nothing more than a one time member of the congregation who had sought his advice. Yet, as they talked, she was conscious of having crossed a threshold of intimacy today and that there was now a frisson between them that had not been there before.

'Would you care for a refill?' Nick, reached for the teapot. 'And another piece of cake, perhaps?'

'Tea, yes. Cake, definitely not.' She held out her mug. 'You know, Nick, I often wonder why you chose to become a priest. Or is that too personal a question?'

'No... Not at all.'

She could see that he was disconcerted by her directness but she felt emboldened to continue.

'This afternoon, for example, when I told you what I found on Jim's computer. Your response wasn't at all what I was expecting.'

'Ah... that's because I wasn't responding as a priest. I felt you wanted my advice as a friend.'

'Yes, and I'm grateful. I was glad you weren't wearing your dog collar today. I couldn't have had that conversation with you if you had been dressed as a priest. I would have found it too inhibiting.'

'Well, I'm a man too, of course...' He was blushing now. 'But I suppose you don't see me like that.'

'Yes, absolutely I see you as a man. It's the priest bit I've never been able to come to terms with. I've always wondered what made you decide to become a priest.'

Nick sighed. 'Well, it's a long story.'

'Then tell me. I'd really like to know.'

'You see that photograph on the mantelpiece?'

'Yes. I was looking at it while you were making the tea. I recognised your younger self, but who is the man with you?'

'That's Tom, my elder brother. He's dead now, sadly.'

'I'm sorry.'

'It was a long time ago. He was only twenty two'

'Did he die in an accident?'

'No, it was a brain tumour. Didn't you know about my brother? I'm sure I told your parents.'

'No, they never mentioned it to me.'

'He was at a seminary training for the priesthood. Tom was five years older than me and I idolized him. We all did - my parents, my younger sister, all of us. He was close to the end of his second year when he came home to give us the news. He had been diagnosed with a malignant tumour and the doctors said they couldn't operate. He thought he had about a year to live. In fact he only lasted five months. It was a terrible time for all of us, watching him go down day by day. Anyway, after his death it was decided that I should take his place, my parents, being the devout Catholics that they are. No, that's unfair. The decision was mine, I could have said no. Had I been a different sort of person I would have done. But I was a very mixed up and immature seventeen year old. And grieving terribly for Tom.' Nick shrugged. 'So, there you have it. I followed in Tom's footsteps and became a priest. Not a very good one, I'm afraid.'

'That's not true.' said Emma. 'You're a very good priest.'

'No, I'm not. Lots of people make the wrong career choice and then have to live with it. Don't misunderstand me. I still get a lot of satisfaction from my work. When I've given comfort to someone who is suffering or grieving perhaps. But it's a lonely life.'

For several seconds Emma was silent. Then she said, 'Do you sometimes wish that you were married and had children?'

'Of course I do. It's my biggest regret. The single life isn't easy, you know, especially for a man. Fortunately celibacy becomes less of a problem with the passing years. Or so they tell me.' He stopped abruptly. 'I'm sorry. I've said too much. Thank you for listening, but perhaps I could ask you not to repeat any of this locally.'

'Of course I won't,' said Emma, getting up. 'Thank you for talking so freely. I feel I know you so much better now.'

'I'm afraid I haven't been much help.'

'But you have. You've been a great help. You've put things into perspective. I needed that.'

As Emma drove home she reflected on her day. On the walk she had been taken aback by Nick's surprisingly liberal attitude towards pornography. Now everything fell into place. Had he told her fifteen years ago of his regret at entering the priesthood, might both their lives have turned out differently? Supposing she had responded by revealing her own feelings. Might she have persuaded him to leave the priesthood and become her lover? There would have been all sorts of obstacles, of course - his parents, the local congregation, the bishop. It would have caused a scandal, certainly, but so what? He could have left the parish and joined her in London to start a new life together.

Noticing the blinking light on the telephone as she entered the hall, she tapped in the code to listen to her voicemail. Two messages. The first was from Sam asking whether she had yet made a decision about New Year. The second message was from Sarah Campion:

Hello Emma, it's Sarah. I called round today in the hope that we might have a pub lunch together. I feel our relationship hasn't got off to a very good start and I would like to try and put that right. Do please call me back. It's best to get me on my mobile 07723 435858. I hope to hear from you soon.

Chapter Fourteen

By the following morning Emma was seeing things more clearly. Thrilling as it would have been to discover that, for twenty years, Nick Hennessy had been as obsessed with her as she was with him, it would have been a short lived gratification. Because then she would find herself reflecting endlessly on what might have been if, all those years ago, she had found the courage to declare her feelings. No, she decided, it was better not to know. For better or worse she was married to Jim and Nick was a priest, albeit a reluctant one.

So, it was a more purposeful and grounded Emma that set off to meet Sarah Campion. This morning she had returned her telephone call declining a lunchtime meeting with the excuse that she had a dental appointment. Which was a lie, of course. She had no desire to become a friend of Sarah Campion and since her plan was simply to confront her with what she knew, lunch was hardly appropriate.

As she entered the coffee shop where they had agreed to meet, Sarah rose immediately to greet her. She looked on edge. 'Hello Emma. Thank you for coming. So you found it all right.'

Emma gave a half smile as she put out her hand. 'Yes, I come to Beaconsfield quite often, actually.'

Sarah beckoned to the waitress. 'What would you like? They do a delicious pan au chocolat. Shall we indulge?'

'Thank you, no. Just black coffee for me.'

Sarah smiled at the waitress. 'Two Americanos please, one with milk.' She turned her attention back to Emma. 'It was so nice to meet you all on Christmas Day. When your father called me I had already resigned myself to spending the whole of Christmas on my own.'

'Yes, he seemed very keen that you should meet us all.'

'And now you're on your own too, I gather. Hasn't Jim flown to America?'

Emma shrugged dismissively. 'Yes, his company is planning a reorganisation. He's in the States to find out where he stands.'

'Does that mean you'll be on your own for New Year?'

'Probably, but it doesn't bother me. Jim is married to his work. We don't see much of each other even when he's at home.'

There was a pause as the waitress brought the coffee. Emma waited until she departed. Then she said 'Tell me, Sarah, how long have you been sleeping with my father?'

Sarah stared at Emma. 'I'm sorry?'

'I know you are sleeping with him, so please do me the courtesy of telling the truth.'

Clearly shocked, it took a while for Sarah to respond. 'Emma, what is this? Why do you suppose your father and I are sleeping together?'

'When I called yesterday, I took the opportunity to go into my father's bedroom.' Emma glared accusingly at Sarah. 'I assume it was your nightdress I found under the pillow.'

A deep blush spread from Sarah's cheeks down to her neck. Then she said quietly, 'Yes, the nightdress was mine.'

'So, he likes black silk, does he? I suppose you have other sexy little numbers for when he gets tired of that one. But, you haven't answered my question.'

Sarah looked at Emma for several seconds. 'Emma, I can understand why you are so upset, but this isn't fair. You have no right to interrogate me like this.'

'Haven't I?' Emma snorted contemptuously. 'First we're told that you and Dad only met in September. Then you admit that you were work colleagues for several years, but barely knew each other. Well, I decided to check on that. And what did I discover? That far from barely knowing him, on at least three occasions you travelled the world together – India, Hong Kong, America. I even came across a photograph of the two of you standing side by side.'

'Yes, I went on some business trips.' Sarah's voice was trembling now. 'But always as a member of a delegation. There were a dozen of us each time, at least.'

'I see. So you didn't get to talk to my father socially on those trips. How long were they - two weeks, three weeks? All the time you only talked business?'

For a moment Sarah didn't answer. Then she said, 'You're quite right, Emma. I did get to know your father when we worked together. I'm just sorry that Patrick chose to handle things the way he did on Christmas Day. We had already agreed to say nothing to anyone, at least until the summer. So, when your father rang to invite me over for a drink, I was worried. So much so that at first I refused his invitation. As I understand it, he was goaded by your brother and said more than he should have done. All right, he didn't tell the truth, but it was with the best of intentions, I assure you.'

'I'm sure it was. The problem is that it now leaves me wondering what else he hasn't told us. That the two of you were sleeping together while my mother was dying of cancer, for instance.'

That absolutely isn't the case.' said Sarah, her voice raised in anger. 'Your father and I were friends. Good friends, but that's all. I don't deny that he confided in me when he and your mother were going through their difficult period a couple of years ago....'

'You mean when my mother's cancer was diagnosed?'

'No. Before that...' Sarah Campion hesitated. 'You obviously don't know about this?'

'I know nothing about any difficult period in my parents' relationship.'

'Then I'm sorry. I'm speaking out of turn.'

'No, tell me. I want to know. I was living in America, remember.'

'I'm sorry. It's not my place to tell you. You must speak to your father.'

'Were you and my father having an affair?'

'No, we weren't having an affair. Not then, or at any time while your mother was still alive. And that's the absolute truth.'

Emma looked at Sarah with contempt. 'But you were in love with him, weren't you?'

Now Sarah's eyes filled with tears. 'Yes, I was in love with your father, almost from the day I met him. But I swear the relationship never developed while we were work colleagues, much as I might have wanted it otherwise. I knew he could never be disloyal to your mother.'

'And you had no contact with him from the time he left the company until three months ago.'

'None.'

Emma gave a sardonic laugh. 'So, setting up your business in High Wycombe and buying a property just a few miles down the road from Dad and then joining his golf club - those decisions were all purely incidental.'

Sarah picked her bag off the floor. 'Of course they weren't. Of course I wanted to see Patrick again. Look, Emma, I think we should end this conversation. I asked to meet you in the hope we could become friends, but I see your feelings are still too raw for that. I'm sorry about the nightdress. That was careless. It shouldn't have happened.' She stood up. 'No, don't get up. Finish your coffee. I'll get the bill on my way out.'

Chapter Fifteen

Lifting her case down from the top of the wardrobe, Emma began assembling the clothes she would take to Sam's for New Year. She knew she had behaved badly towards Sarah yesterday and spent the rest of the day wishing she hadn't agreed to meet her so soon. Because, what had she achieved? Dad was hardly going to end the relationship because of her disapproval. As Sam had said, it was no business of hers whom Dad chose to spend his time with, or sleep with, for that matter.

Carrying her case downstairs she put it by the front door. Could she trust Sarah's word that the relationship began only after Mum died? She had given that a good deal of thought over the past twenty four hours and had to concede that she was probably telling the truth. But what did she mean by Dad going through a 'difficult period' even before the cancer was diagnosed? Saskia said something similar the other day, though she couldn't remember what exactly. Had there been problems in the marriage that she was unaware of?

She switched on her phone to find three text messages, all of them from Jim. Where was she? Why wasn't she answering? He was only available until 5.00pm, her time. Call him soon, please, he was missing her. The last message was accompanied by half a dozen kisses. Tapping in his number, he answered almost immediately.

'Hello Em. Sorry about all the messages, but I was beginning to get worried.'

'No, it's my fault. I should have phoned sooner. How's it going?'

'I'm not sure. I think we're making progress.'

'How was your presentation?'

'It went okay, but you never really know, do you? What about you? What have you been doing?....'

Emma told Jim about calling on her father, but made no mention of the nightdress. Nor did she mention her encounter with Sarah, or what she had discovered on his computer. But she did tell him about meeting Nick on Coombe Hill and their walk together back down to Wendover.

'What did you talk about?'

'Oh, this and that. Nothing in particular.'

'I miss you, Em. You know that, don't you. I know I'm not much good at saying such things, but I do miss you.'

'You'll be home soon,' said Emma, softening her voice a little. She wasn't used to displays of affection from Jim.

'Talk tomorrow?'

'Yes. I'll be at Sam's. He's invited me for New Year.'

Ending the call she was glad she hadn't mentioned the pornography. Nor would she when he came home. Nick was right. For too long she had been so obsessed with conceiving a child that their lovemaking must have seemed more a duty than a pleasure. She resolved to be more attentive in future.

Emma carried her case outside to her car. It was kind of Sam to invite her for New Year, though she would really have preferred to stay at home. She might even have given Nick a call, inviting him to join her for a New Year's Eve meal. She could still do that, of course. She could still back out of Sam's invitation, pleading illness.

Tapping in Nick's number she could feel her heart pounding as she waited for him to answer.

'Hello. Nick Hennessy speaking.'

'Hi Nick... It's Emma.'

'Emma! How nice to hear your voice. Do you know, I was about to ring you. I've been feeling badly about telling you of my miseries when you are going through such a worrying time yourself.'

'Not at all. It was kind of you to walk with me and listen while I poured out my troubles.'

'Do you feel better today?'

'I do. And thank you. I realise now I had no business going through Jim's computer files in the first place.'

'Even so, what you found must have come as quite a shock. But I really wouldn't worry too much about Jim.'

Emma took a deep breath. Should she invite him? No, it would be wrong. 'What are you doing at New Year, Nick?'

'Oh, I don't know. Probably a bit of television, followed by an early night. How about you?'

'Sam and Zoe have invited me to spend it with them.'

'That's nice. It had occurred to me that, since you were on your own, you might join me for an early supper.'

'Really? I would have liked that.'

'A pity. Another time perhaps.'

Disappointed as she was, Emma tried to be positive as she set off in the direction of Solihull. Joining Nick for a New Year supper would have been an awkward encounter. Since she would be driving, she would only be able to have one glass of wine at most - hardly enough to loosen any inhibitions on her part. Or on his, since he would feel the need to match her restraint. No, perhaps it was better that she was going to Sam's after all.

Pressing her foot down hard she moved into the fast lane. She had to get Nick Hennessy out of her head? It was all water under the bridge. If ever he'd had feelings for her, they belonged to a time long past. No, they had each made their choices and would have to live with them.

Chapter Sixteen

Sam's house was as cramped and over furnished as on Emma's last visit, but at least someone, probably Zoe, had gone to the trouble of putting flowers in her bedroom and clearing some space in the wardrobe. After freshening up she came downstairs.

'Drink, after your long drive?' said Sam, coming into the sitting room with a bottle of wine and two glasses.

'I'll just have a fruit juice, thanks.'

Sam set the glasses down on the table and unscrewed the bottle. 'Come on, you're not driving anywhere tonight. Have a proper drink.'

'Very well. But just a small one.'

'Not sure if I know how to pour a small one,' he said, filling her glass.

'No, no. That's far too much. I only want half that amount.'

'Relax. Leave what you can't drink.'

Zoe, wearing a frilly pink apron, came in from the kitchen with a glass of orange juice 'The meal won't be long. Cheers everyone. It's lovely to see you, Emma.'

'It's nice of you to invite me,' said Emma as they clinked glasses.

Zoe sat down next to Sam. 'I do think you have lovely hair, Emma. Doesn't she, Sam? I wish I had nice thick hair like yours. Have you ever thought of having it re-styled? I've got my scissors with me if you'd like to experiment.'

'I'm quite happy with my hair the way it is, thank you, Zoe,' Emma replied primly.

Blushing, Zoe got up. 'I'll just go and check the recipe again. I haven't done this meal before, you see.'

As she returned to the kitchen Sam grinned at Emma. 'The truth is she hasn't actually done any meal before. Normally I do the cooking.'

'I'm sure it will be very nice,' said Emma, feeling a little guilty at the way she had rejected Zoe's offer. 'Shall I go and give her a hand?'

'No. Leave her. She'll only get in a muddle.' He refilled his glass. 'So, New Year, Em. There'll be eleven of us altogether.'

'Eleven! I thought you said you were having a quiet New Year with just the three of us.'

'I know, but on second thoughts, I decided it might be a bit dull. They're just some of the neighbours, plus two girls from the salon with their partners. I haven't met them myself yet.'

'You might have told me, Sam,' said Emma, confounded by the sudden change of plan. 'I haven't brought anything I can wear for a big party.'

'Don't worry about it. You'll be fine.' Sam reached for the bottle and topped up her glass. 'You can always pop into town tomorrow if you're not happy. Zoe will go with you.'

By the time they sat down at the small circular dining table in the window, Emma was feeling more relaxed, although she was conscious that she had had more to drink than she was used to. The chicken was overcooked, but she was flattered by the care Zoe had taken over it and made a point of complimenting her on producing such a delicious meal.

'Would you like some coffee, Emma?' Zoe was on her feet before Emma could respond.

'Thank you. That would be very nice.'

'Leave the coffee for now, Sweetie,' said Sam. 'We haven't finished the bottle yet.'

'No Sam, please,' said Emma who was beginning to feel a little woozy. 'I don't want any more. I'm not used to it. It will make me ill.'

'Come on, the last drop'.

'No. You mustn't make me. Zoe's not drinking.'

'Ah, well there's a reason for that.' He gave Zoe a sly smile. 'Shall we tell her, Sweets?'

'I think it's a bit soon, Sam,' said Zoe. 'Shouldn't we wait?'

'Yes, but Emma is family, after all.' Pulling Zoe towards him he put his arm round her. 'Zoe's pregnant.'

'It's only a home test,' said Zoe, beaming at Sam. 'I'll need to have a scan to be sure.'

For a moment Emma could think of nothing to say. 'But I thought the two of you only met just before ....'

Zoe laughed nervously. 'I know, I know. That's what I said to Sam. We don't waste much time, do we? And I don't know how it's happened. Because we were taking precautions, weren't we, Sam?'

Sam gave Zoe a hug. 'Actually, Em I think it's best if you keep it under your hat for the time being. Tell Jim by all means, but don't say anything to Dad. We'll get to twelve weeks. Then we'll tell him ourselves.'

'Do you think he'll be excited, Emma?' said Zoe. 'I mean, about being a granddad again. We're hoping it's a girl aren't we, Sam. Sam wants a girl. because he's got a little boy already. But I don't mind either way so long as it's got all its bits. Do you think your Dad would like it to be a girl, Emma?'

'I really have no idea.' said Emma, still at a loss for words.

'Oh, I do think your Dad's a lovely man, Emma.' said Zoe, 'and so dishy too. I can see where Sam gets his good looks from. I bet he was a real one for the ladies when he was younger. Like his son, I think. But isn't it nice that he and Sarah are such good friends? I thought she was lovely. Very refined, but not a bit stuck up. Don't you think so, Emma?'

'I can't say' said Emma stiffly. 'I didn't talk to her a great deal'.

'And your Jim, he's lovely too. I have to admit I was a bit unsure of him at first. I said so, didn't I Sam? Because he was so quiet. But I always say with quiet people, there's usually a lot more there than meets the eye. And when I got him talking he was really nice and lots of fun.'

'Yes, he's all right is Gentleman Jim,' said Sam, gently easing Zoe off his knee and back into her chair. 'Maybe you two should think about starting a family, Em. It shouldn't be left entirely to me to supply the grandchildren.'

'Thank you, Sam. I'll bear it in mind.'

'I'm only sorry that I couldn't have met your Mum,' continued Zoe, 'because I'm sure she must have been a lovely person too. You all made me feel so special at Christmas that I feel part of the family already....'

Zoe stopped in mid sentence when she saw that Emma was crying.

Sam moved awkwardly towards her and squeezed her arm. 'Come on Em, lighten up....'

Emma took out a tissue and blew her nose hard. 'I'm sorry, Zoe but I just don't recognise my family from the way you describe them. For a start, whatever else my father is, he is certainly not a lovely person, although you are right, unfortunately, about him being one for the ladies and I don't think that was necessarily confined to his younger days. As for Sarah I don't think she's lovely at all. You and Sam may think it is perfectly all right for the two of them to be in a relationship so soon after our mother's death, but I don't. As for Jim ... I think the less I say about Jim the better. In fact the only person you are right about in your charming little eulogy is our mother, who was in fact as lovely and loving a person as you describe, except that you didn't actually know her, did you Zoe, so I don't know how you can possibly comment.'

At this Zoe too burst into tears and ran out of the room, followed quickly by Sam, leaving Emma to ponder on the damage done by her sudden outburst. A minute or so later she heard Sam coming downstairs.

'I'm sorry, Sam. I shouldn't have said those things. Shall I go up to her?'

Sam sighed resignedly. 'No. Leave her be. She'll be fine in the morning'

'I'm afraid the news of her pregnancy tipped me over the edge.'

'Really?'

As her eyes filled again with tears, Emma took out a tissue, 'We've been trying for five years, Sam. Five long years.'

Sam sat down next to her. 'Sorry. If I'd known, we wouldn't have told you. Yes it was a bit of a shock for me too when Zoe delivered the glad tidings. Still, it's done now. No use crying over spilt milk.' He put his hand on hers. 'I know you think she's an airhead, Em and wonder what the hell I see in her. But, she's a good kid. She's kind and generous and there's no side to her. I know everyone thought Saskia was wonderful and the best thing that could have happened to me. But I'm not like you. I'm a simple soul. Saskia was too smart for me, too clever. I needed someone who likes me the way I am, not someone who makes me feel inferior.'

Emma didn't answer.

'Come on girl. I think we should all go to bed.'

Chapter Seventeen

Sam was clearing up from last night's dinner when Emma came downstairs. She'd had a troubled night, partly the result of drinking too much, but also because she was conscience stricken at her unprovoked attack on Zoe.

'Hi, Em. Sleep well?'
'Not particularly.'
'Coffee?'
'Thank you. I'll do it.' Emma filled the kettle and switched it on. 'Is Zoe up yet?'
'Yes, she was up before me. She's gone out'.
'Oh? Where to?'
'No idea. Do you want cereal?'
'Coffee's fine. Can I make you some?'
'Not for me.'

Emma made her coffee and brought it over to the table. 'I'm really sorry about last night, Sam. I seem to be upsetting everyone at the moment.'

'Really?' Sam switched on the dishwasher and closed the door.

'First Dad, then Sarah and now Zoe.'

'I knew you'd upset Dad. I didn't know about Sarah? When was this?'

'On Thursday. She rang suggesting we meet. She said she felt our relationship hadn't got off to a good start and she wanted to try and clear the air. You were right. I should have kept out of it. It's none of my business.'

'What did you say to her?'

'I'm afraid I was pretty hostile. I practically accused her of being a whore.'

'Strong stuff. Was this at her house?'

'No. In a cafe in Beaconsfield.'

'You might have chosen somewhere more private. What did you say to her? She seemed a nice enough person to me.'

'I know, I know. But Dad lied to us. She's sleeping with him, Sam. She's sleeping with him already.'

'She told you that, did she?'

'Of course she didn't. It was when I called on Dad on Tuesday. I made an excuse to go upstairs. I know it was wrong of me, but I couldn't help myself. I went into Dad's bedroom and looked under the pillow on Mum's side of the bed. There was a nightdress there. It was hers.'

'I see. So you confronted her with your discovery, did you?'

'Yes.'

'And did she admit it? That they're sleeping together?'

'Not in so many words, but she could hardly deny it.'

Sam gave a long sigh 'Listen Em, I know I keep saying this, but what Dad does with his life has nothing to do with us. Why shouldn't they be sleeping together? He's only sixty. Do you want him to spend the rest of his life living like a hermit?'

'Of course not. It just seems so premature, that's all. What does it say about their marriage, Sam, that he's sleeping with another woman already? And in the very bed he and Mum slept in for nearly forty years. I thought they had a happy marriage.'

'Happy?' Sam shrugged. 'Yes, I suppose it was happy enough, as marriages go. But I would hardly describe it as a marriage made in heaven.'

'Really? What makes you say that?'

Sam sat down facing her. "Have you ever wondered why we never saw much of Granny and Grandad Kinsella when we were growing up?

'I always assumed it was because they couldn't leave the farm.'

'Or why Mum didn't finish her degree course? I mean, people get over glandular fever, don't they? She could have gone back to university.'

'That's because she had a nervous breakdown of some kind.'

'Do you really believe that? Let me ask you another. Why are there no photographs of Mum and Dad's wedding?'

'Mum always said it was a quiet wedding because Granny and Grandad didn't approve of her marrying a non Catholic.'

'True, but the real reason there are no photographs is because Mum was already six months pregnant. With me. They didn't get married in 1978 as we were always led to believe. The wedding was a year later in 1979, by which time I was well on the way,'

Emma shook her head. 'Sam, why are you telling me all this?'

'Why I'm telling you is because Mum and Dad didn't marry for love. They got married because they were made to, by Grandad Kinsella. It's what they used to call a shotgun wedding. Still is in parts of rural Ireland.'

'But this is the late seventies we're talking about, not the dark ages. Surely attitudes were more liberal by then, even in Ireland.'

'Not as far as Granny and Grandad were concerned. To them a child conceived out of wedlock wasn't just a mortal sin, it brought shame on the whole family.'

'Who told you all this?' said Emma, still not wanting to believe Sam's story.

'I'd always had my suspicions. So, one weekend about five years ago I decided to go and see Mum's Aunt Alice. I thought if anyone would tell me the truth, she would, being something of an outcast herself for marrying a Protestant. It wasn't long before I had her giving me chapter and verse, confirming everything I'd always suspected. Mum's parents never forgave Dad for getting her pregnant, or Mum for letting it happen.'

'So they forced them to get married. Is that what you're saying?'

'Auntie Alice said they weren't even going out together by the time Mum discovered she was pregnant. Grandad Kinsella was furious. He was all for throwing Mum out, disowning her completely. If it wasn't for Granny's intervention, she thinks he would have done. In the end Grandad Kinsella arranged a meeting with Dad and persuaded him to do the right thing by their daughter. Auntie Alice even thinks some money changed hands, but she's not sure about that. Anyway, it seems Dad agreed because, within weeks, Grandad had arranged a hushed up wedding in some remote village church where no one knew them. Then they were packed them off to England to stay with Dad's family until the birth. Yes, a lot of things became clearer to me after talking to Auntie Alice.'

'Like what?'

'Like the reason Mum never loved me like she loved you.'

'How can you say that?' scoffed Emma. 'She loved us both equally.'

'No Em, she didn't. I was never good enough, was I? Always a disappointment. Left school without any O'levels, quit the army at the first opportunity, failed to get a decent career, failed even in my marriage. Unlike his sweet biddable younger sister who could do no wrong. No, I was the living reminder of Mum's wicked fall from grace and she never got over it.'

'Come on, Sam, you're reading too much into this. She loved you just as much as me. And just because they had to get married, that doesn't mean the marriage was unhappy.'

'I'm telling you, Em, Mum never forgave herself for getting pregnant outside marriage. I think it explains why she got so involved with the Church, going to Mass every day and confession every Saturday. Even a lifetime of penitence couldn't wash away the guilt.'

Emma studied her brother. 'Tell me, Sam, since you seem to know so much. Did something happen between Mum and Nick Hennessy while Jim and I were in America?'

'Between Mum and Father Nick? What makes you think that?'

'It was something Sarah Campion said the other day. And Saskia hinted at it too when I saw her on Boxing Day. About Mum and Dad going through a difficult time in their marriage. About Dad being at his wit's end.'

Sam gave a long sigh. 'Yes, I suppose you have a right to the truth. You're right. Something did happen between Mum and Nick Hennessy. Dad didn't want you to know. I think he would have preferred that I didn't know either, but

I was living back home by then, so he could hardly keep it from me.'

'Saskia wouldn't talk about it. She said I should ask you.'

'Okay, if you really want to know. It all started about four years ago. Just after you and Jim went off to Los Angeles. We hardly noticed anything at first. Just that Mum seemed to be getting more and more involved with St Josephs. You know, putting herself on the cleaning rota, arranging the flowers, taking the Sunday School, things like that. And she even started going to Mass on weekdays as well as Sundays and to confession every Saturday. Then the rumours started. Some woman in the congregation telephoned Dad saying Mum was being over familiar with Nick and people were starting to talk.'

'Did he speak to Mum about it?'

'Not at first. Dad thought the woman was just making mischief. But then we both noticed that Mum seemed to be developing a fixation on Nick, constantly talking about him, singing his praises, finding reasons to visit him at the presbytery. Meanwhile, she wasn't getting at all well with Dad. Always criticising him and putting him down. She even stopped sleeping with him on the pretext that his snoring kept her awake. I wasn't aware that Dad did snore, but that was the excuse she gave.'

'Didn't Dad challenge her about the way she was behaving?'

'He tried. We both did. But she refused to accept there was anything amiss. Then, one day Dad told me he was going to see Nick and have the whole thing out. He never told me what took place between them, but it certainly knocked it on the head. Because, a couple of days later, came the big fall out. In the space of a weekend, Mum went from being Nick's number one fan, to denouncing him as a fraud and an imposter whom she didn't want within a mile of the house and never wanted to speak to again. It was the same weekend that she abandoned St Josephs and her Catholic faith. Then her test results came through and we had bigger things to worry about.'

'Do you think Mum and Nick were actually having an affair?'

'I don't know about that. I'm not sure Dad does either. But there's no doubt Mum was obsessed with Nick. Whether it was a full blown affair, only he can tell you.'

Emma sat for a long time without speaking. Then she said, 'Sam, I'm sorry, but do you mind if I don't stay for New Year. What you've just told me has come as quite a shock. I need some time to process it.'

'Then, you won't stay to see Zoe?'

'No, I'll go now. Tell her I'll write.'

'Wait at least until she comes back. She'll be sorry not to say goodbye.'

'No. If you don't mind, I'd rather go now. I'll just get my things together.'

Five minutes later Emma came downstairs with her suitcase and took it out to her car. As she was opening the boot Zoe came into the drive carrying a bunch of flowers. She looked as if she had been crying.

'Emma's decided to go home, Sweetie,' said Sam coming out to meet her. 'She's not feeling too well'

Emma turned to Zoe. 'Zoe, I want to apologise for the things I said last night. I'm afraid I was a little overwrought, but...'

'No, please don't go Emma,' said Zoe, the tears running down her cheeks. 'It's me that needs to apologise. That's why I went out. I'm so sorry to upset you. Sam's always telling me about my prattling on. I should have realised..... Anyway I got you some flowers in the hope we can still be friends....'

As Emma took the flowers from her, she too burst into tears. 'Of course we can.... That's very kind Zoe. I'm sorry. I can't talk. I'll write, I promise.' She turned to Sam and hugged him. 'Goodbye Sam and thank you. Thank you both.'

Chapter Eighteen

Emma was so consumed by Sam's revelations that she was barely aware of the drive home. It had never occurred to her that her mother's failure to complete her university degree was for reasons other than illness. Nor had she ever wondered why there were no photographs of her parents wedding. As for never seeing Granny and Grandad Kinsella throughout their childhood, she had always accepted that Ireland was too costly for them to visit as a family and her grandparents couldn't visit them because they couldn't leave the farm.

She had been unbelievably blinkered, she realised that now. Her parents marriage was happy because that was how she wanted it to be. If there were frictions, particularly in the early years, it was Sam's fault, not theirs. As for Mum's religious faith, yes, it did get a bit intense as she got older, but that was a legacy from her strict upbringing.

Now, thanks to Sam, she would have to come to terms with a very different version of her parents' relationship. It was a marriage founded on guilt, a union riddled with resentment and recrimination. Nor, it seems, did they find happiness and contentment in those final years, before her mother's illness took over their lives. Because, according to Sam, that was the worst time of all - a time when their relationship was so bad that they weren't even sleeping in the same room. But was her mother unfaithful? The idea of her committing adultery with any man seemed hardly likely, but to have done so with a priest, a man sworn to celibacy, seemed almost beyond belief.

As she turned into the drive she was surprised to see her father's car parked in front of the garage, her father at the wheel. As she pulled in beside him he got out, his face taut with anger.

'Hello Dad, what are you doing here?' she said brightly as she stepped out of the car.

'Waiting for you. That's what I'm doing. I thought you were going to spend New Year with Sam and Zoe.'

'I was,' she said, closing the door. 'But they decided to have a party. I'm not up to parties right now.'

'So Sam tells me. They're very upset that you walked out on them, Zoe particularly. I hope you know that.'

'It's just that I've got rather a lot on my mind at the moment,' she said, taking the house keys from her bag. 'Shall we go inside?'

Patrick followed her indoors and into the sitting room.

'Do you want a cup of tea? Or a drink? There isn't much in the house at the moment, I'm afraid.'

'Nothing, thank you.' He sat down facing her, his eyes fixed on hers. 'Emma, you had no right to speak to Sarah as you did yesterday. She's blameless in all this, do you hear me? And while we're on the subject, I was extremely cross to learn that you've been snooping round my bedroom and looking under pillows. I wouldn't dream of doing such a thing in your house, even though you are my daughter.'

Emma felt herself reddening. 'I know, Dad and I'm sorry. But can't you see why I did it? First you tell everyone that you and Sarah only met after Mum died. Then you admit that you were work colleagues but your paths rarely crossed. Which seemed unlikely, since she was the marketing manager of your largest subsidiary. So,

I did a bit of research when I got home and what did I discover? That far from your paths rarely crossing, she was part of your sales delegation on at least three of your overseas business trips. Are you telling me you only ever talked shop during all those evenings staying in hotels on the other side of the world?'

Patrick sighed. 'All right, Emma, cool down. Yes, I did lie. But Sarah isn't the femme fatale you believe her to be. It's true that she and I were good friends before your mother died, but the relationship never went further, I swear. It was stupid of me to mention her at all over Christmas, let alone invite her for drinks. She was all for waiting another six months at least. But you know how it is. When Sam began quizzing me, there was one part of me remembering Sarah's advice and another for getting it all out in the open. I ended up steering a course between the two and messed things up completely.'

'The thing I can't get my head round, Dad, is that you felt able to sleep with her in the same bed Mum slept in. I'm sorry but it seems so disrespectful to her memory. And I always thought you and Mum were happy...'

'We were happy, Em. I miss your mother very much, as I'm sure you do.'

'Even though you and Mum were made to get married because you got Mum pregnant. Which was the real reason she didn't finish her university course.'

Patrick stiffened. 'Who told you that?'

'Sam told me. He went to see Auntie Alice after you scuppered my idea for a twenty fifth wedding anniversary party. You got married in 1979, didn't you, not in 1978 as you had us all believe.'

Patrick shook his head wearily. 'Yes, we got married in 1979. I was all for telling you the truth, but your mother wouldn't hear of it.'

'Why not? We were both adults by then, for God's sake.'

'Because she insisted on keeping it a secret. For Sam's sake. She wanted to protect Sam.'

'Protect Sam? Protect him from what? I know there used to be a stigma about getting pregnant outside marriage, but not in the late seventies, surely.'

'I'm afraid there was as far as your mother was concerned. She believed she committed a grave sin getting pregnant and she didn't want Sam to get the idea he was an unwanted child. And Sam wasn't easy, as you well know. Your mother was always very strict with him. Too strict, in my opinion. It was as if she was punishing him for her own sin. While I was probably too soft as I tried to make it up to him. With the consequence that he played us one off against the other, as children do.'

'Yes, I knew Sam was difficult,' said Emma, 'but I always thought you and Mum were happy. I never thought there was any friction between you.'

'Oh, there was friction all right. Though the worst times were in the first few years, before you came along. And again after you left home. The truth is your mother resented being made to marry me in the first place. Hard as I tried to make it up to her, she never forgave me for interrupting her degree course and ruining her chances of a career. Things got easier when you arrived. You were such an easy child, compared with Sam. While you were at home you brought us together.'

Emma got up and walked over to the window. It was starting to snow. Thick fluffy snowflakes fell against the window, sliding down the pane as they melted.

'Sam told me a lot more, Dad. He said that in the last few years, when he was back living at home, you and Mum were barely speaking to one another. Is that true?'

'I'm afraid it is. You were in Los Angeles, of course, so we both tried to put on a brave face when you telephoned. But it was a difficult time.'

He said there were even rumours going round that Mum was having an affair with Nick Hennessy and ...'

'There was no evidence for that,' said Patrick, interrupting her sharply. 'None at all. It was just silly tittle tattle.'

Emma came and sat down again. 'But you went to see Nick, didn't you? What for?'

Patrick hesitated before answering. 'The truth is, I believed at the time that your mother was mentally ill. She never got over the guilt of her pregnancy, or the shame it brought on her family. Her parents didn't make it any easier, of course, being the devout Irish Catholics that they were. I went to see Nick because I thought her involvement with the Church was becoming obsessive.'

'And she was also visiting Nick at the presbytery, wasn't she?'

'She was. There's no doubt that she had developed some kind of an obsession for him. They weren't having an affair though, I'm sure about that.'

'So, what did she visit him there for, if they weren't having an affair?'

'According to Nick they just talked, endlessly. And argued. He said she became very emotional sometimes.'

'About what?'

'About everything. She talked a good deal about her 'mortal sin', as she described it, and of its consequences. Being cast out by her family, having to step down from her degree course, being made to marry me, the problems we had raising Sam.'

As Patrick looked away Emma saw there were tears in his eyes.

'Dad, would you have married Mum if you hadn't got her pregnant?'

Patrick shook his head. 'I suppose the answer to that is no. After all, we weren't even going out together when I got her letter giving me the bad news.'

'And then Grandad came to see you.'

'He did. And it was a pretty unnerving experience, I can tell you. You may have thought Grandad was a fearsome enough individual when you knew him, but that was nothing compared to how he was when I first met him. Frightened the life out of me, he did.'

'So, but for Grandad putting on the pressure, you wouldn't have married Mum. Is that what you're saying?'

'I suppose I am saying that, yes. But then your mother wouldn't have married me, would she?'

'Are you so sure about that? After all, she let you get her pregnant.'

'No. I take full responsibility for getting her pregnant. You have to remember that your mother was a pretty naive eighteen year old when I met her. Whereas I was anything but naive. No, I wasn't at all the sort of person your mother would have chosen, given a free choice.'

'Really?'

'For a start, she would have preferred, at least, to marry a practising Christian, if not a Roman Catholic. I was also something of a philistine, wasn't I, compared to her. She loved reading, music, theatre, the arts, whereas I preferred sport, partying, socialising - all the things she hated. Oh, I tried to make her happy. And there were times I thought I'd succeeded, but it was never for long. The best time was when you came along. For once we had something we could share, something to bring us together.'

'I'm so sorry, Dad.' Now there were tears in her own eyes as Emma got up and went over to join him on the sofa. 'Can you forgive me for being so stupid and cruel. I mean both of you. Will Sarah ever forgive me?'

Patrick put his arm round his daughter. 'Of course she'll forgive you. I promise she will. She always knew it was going to be a bumpy ride.'

Chapter Nineteen

There was a light scattering of snow on the morning of New Years Eve as Emma set off for Princes Risborough. She had spent yesterday evening in brooding contemplation, before going to bed early. But, with so much going on in her mind, she couldn't get to sleep. After a couple of hours she gave up and came downstairs to spend the next two hours writing letters, firstly to her father, then to Sarah and finally to Zoe and Sam to apologise for her unacceptable behaviour of the past few days.

Now she had one last piece of unfinished business to attend to. Whatever hurt it might cause her, she had to get to the truth about her mother's relationship with Nick Hennessy. Parking outside the presbytery she walked nervously up to the front door and rang the bell. What would he say when she confronted him? Would he tell the truth, or would he lie? Perhaps it would be better if he lied. Because, if the truth was what she believed it to be, she wasn't sure how she would cope. The thought of Nick taking advantage of her mother's vulnerability was too awful to contemplate.

'Emma!'

As Nick opened the door he seemed both surprised and pleased to see her. Thankfully he wasn't wearing his dog collar, but was dressed casually in jeans and a polo necked sweater.

'But I thought you were at Sam's for New Year.'

'I know. I decided not to stay after all.'

'Come in, come in.' Turning, he led her into the sitting room.

'I've come for some answers, Nick, about you and my mother...' She stopped abruptly. She was speaking too quickly and needed to slow down. 'What I mean is...I've learned a great deal in the last few days that I knew absolutely nothing about. I decided that only you can give me the full story.'

'I'll certainly try,' said Nick sitting down opposite her. 'But first, can I get you some coffee, or tea?'

She shook her head. 'I had a long talk with Sam yesterday and then with Dad. I gather the reason Mum dropped out of university wasn't because she had glandular fever, as we'd always been led to believe, but because she was pregnant. They only got married at all because Mum's parents forced them to. Did you know any of this?'

Nick hesitated a moment before answering. 'Yes, I did know. Your mother told me in confidence a long time ago. But that doesn't mean they weren't happy together, Emma. I believe they loved one another very much.'

'Do you really think so? Do you really believe that?'

'I do. As for the circumstances of their wedding, I know it's hard to believe, but a pregnancy outside marriage was still a shameful thing in parts of Ireland, even as late as the nineteen seventies. I'm afraid your mother never really got over the guilt of that pregnancy. I believe it haunted her until the day she died.'

'Was that why she kept it a secret from Sam and me?'

'It was absolutely the reason. They neither of them wanted Sam to think he was an unwanted child. Which I'm sure he wasn't, once everyone got over the trauma of the pregnancy.'

Emma sighed. 'And I'd always thought Mum and Dad had a happy marriage.'

'I'm sure they did. As you know, your parents were very different people, but it's certainly my impression that they were happy together.'

'Really? Because that's not the only thing Sam told me. He said that after Jim and I left for Los Angeles, rumours were going round the village that you and Mum were having an affair. And that Dad was so concerned that he came to see you about it.'

Nick looked uneasily at Emma. 'Has your father never mentioned any of this to you?'

'No. Not until yesterday. I suppose he only confided in Sam because he was living at home at the time and would have heard the rumours for himself.'

'Well, it's true that your father came to see me, but it certainly wasn't to accuse me. He told me he was becoming increasingly concerned about your mother's mental state. Specifically he was worried that her religious faith was turning into an obsession. I agreed. By then hardly a day went by without her finding some reason to visit St Josephs.'

'Or you, here at the presbytery.'

Nick flinched. 'Yes, that too.'

'Tell me then. Were you and Mum having an affair?'

For several seconds Nick simply looked at Emma. 'If you mean, did we have sex, the answer is no.'

'But you kissed and embraced. Is that what you're saying?'

Nick shook his head wearily. 'Emma, you have to believe this. I never tried to seduce your mother. I don't deny that my thoughts were sometimes less pure than my actions, but I knew she was vulnerable and that it would have been wrong to take advantage of her vulnerability even if I wasn't a priest. I suspected that her obsession with the Church and with me in particular, was driven by her need to find absolution. I suppose in her eyes I had become a kind of Jesus figure to her Mary Magdalene. I know that sounds trite, but it's the only way I can explain it.'

Emma fell silent. Did she believe him? Was he telling her the truth?

'I admit I was at fault, Emma. I should have heeded the warning signals earlier.'

'How did Mum behave towards you?'

'When she first came to see me here at the presbytery, she was quite withdrawn and I did what I could to comfort and reassure her. It was only later, and gradually, that I realised she was...'

'Falling in love with you?'

'You could call it that, but I knew it wasn't love. I knew I needed to be on my guard.'

'Did she make sexual advances?'

'Emma, I don't pretend that I was innocent in all this. I knew I should have discouraged her visits, or at least seen her in public places rather than here. The truth is I was lonely and I was flattered by her attentions. I can't honestly say what I might have done, if your father hadn't come to see me when he did.'

'What did Dad say to you, if he didn't accuse you?'

'He asked me if there was anything I could do to help. I said I would find a way to deal with it. Which I did.'

'How?'

'Do I have to tell you?' There were tears now in Nick's eyes. 'I fear that if I tell you the truth I will lose your trust and friendship just as I did your mother's. I don't think I could bear that.'

Emma looked steadily at Nick. 'You won't lose my friendship, Nick, I promise.'

'You see, the truth is, I'm an imposter, Emma. Although I continue to work as a priest, I no longer believe in God, not in a caring God anyway. Nor do I believe in the teachings of the Catholic Church.'

Emma stared at Nick in incredulity. 'I'm shocked.'

'Yes. Your mother was shocked too when I told her.'

'How did she react?'

'Badly. As I knew she would. But that was my intention.'

'Are you telling me, Nick, that for twenty years you've carried out your duties as a priest, even though you don't even believe in God?'

'I'm not alone in this, Emma, believe me. Losing one's faith isn't unknown, even within the priesthood.'

'Then you don't believe in Jesus, or the resurrection.'

'I believe in Jesus as a historical figure, but not as the son of God. I also believe he was crucified, but not that he rose again from the dead.'

'So, you don't believe in salvation, or the afterlife.'

'Please don't judge me too harshly, Emma. I still get satisfaction from my work and I continue to do it to the best of my ability. But, if I had my time over again I wouldn't have become a priest.'

Emma looked away. 'I'm sorry. I don't know what to say.'

'I knew that by telling your mother the truth I risked undermining her own faith.'

'Maybe you did. Mum never spoke about God or an afterlife in all the time she was ill. Not even when she knew she was dying.'

'Then I'm truly sorry about that.'

'I still don't understand why she couldn't tell me the truth, instead of leaving everything shrouded in mystery.'

'I can explain that. Neither of your parents wanted you to know the truth. They thought that if they told you I was a non believer, it might undermine your own faith and they didn't want to risk that. Not just your mother, your father too. And they were concerned for my parishioners. It would hardly have looked good if word got round that their parish priest no longer believed in God.'

Emma sat in silence for a few moments, then she stood up. 'Thank you, Nick. I understand everything now.'

Nick got up too. 'And now you despise me too, don't you?'

'No. I view you differently, that's all.'

'Then I haven't undermined your own faith. I hope I haven't'

'You haven't. I just feel sorry for you.'

'Yes. It's a terrible thing to lose one's faith. I keep telling myself that if I keep working at it, one day it will return.'

'I hope it will.' Emma turned and walked slowly out into the hall.'

'When does Jim get back?' said Nick, following her to the door.

'I don't know yet. He'll probably be there a few more days.'

'So, you're by yourself for New Year after all.'

'Yes.'

Nick hesitated. 'Then...would you care to join me for a meal? If you can trust my cooking, that is. Or, if you prefer, we could go to a restaurant.'

Emma smiled. 'Yes, a meal would be very nice.'

'Which is it to be then? A restaurant, or would you like to come here?'

Now it was Emma who hesitated. Which was it to be? A restaurant would be safer, but then...'Thank you, Nick. I think I would prefer to come here.'

Chapter Twenty

'Can I tempt you to a glass of Champagne?'

Emma gave Nick a cautious smile. 'Thank you. Perhaps one glass won't do me any harm.'

She had arrived in a state of guilty anticipation, in spite of telling herself she was doing nothing wrong. Why shouldn't she have supper with a family friend? Although this morning, driving home, she had been less sure. If Nick had lost his faith, surely the honourable course of action was to resign from the priesthood and find another occupation. So, why hadn't he? Was he afraid of how people would react - his bishop, his parents, the congregation? Or was it because he was scared of the big wide world he would be entering?

By lunchtime her views had softened. Nick regretted losing his faith and said he wished he could find it again. So, what better way to regain it than by serving the congregation entrusted to him and continuing his life of self denial. Far from being a fraud and an imposter, he was to be admired for the sacrifice he was making. She should count herself fortunate to have such an admirable person for a friend.

Satisfied that in accepting his offer she had made the right decision, she spent the next hour or more going through her wardrobe deciding what to wear. A slim chiffon tunic top with black leggings was her first choice but, in the end, she decided that might be too provocative. In the end she decided on a simple white blouse and black trousers as more suitable for the occasion. After showering she then sat at her dressing table, curling her hair with a hot brush she hadn't used in years and experimenting with eyeliners and different shades of lipstick until she found the combination she liked best.

'Here we are,' said Nick, returning with the wine. 'The glasses are quite small, so I don't think you need worry about being over the limit. Cheers.'

They clinked glasses and he sat down on the opposite side of the fireplace facing her.

'Thank you for inviting me tonight, Nick. I wasn't looking forward to spending the evening on my own. Though I suppose, after twenty years, you're used to your own company.'

'Not at all. In my experience the loneliness gets worse, not better. Having a dog helps. If it wasn't for old Bob here, I think I might have gone mad by now.'

Pricking up his ears at the sound of his name, the Labrador gave his master an enquiring glance, yawned and stretched, before settling down again in front of the fire.

'You've had him a long time, haven't you?' said Emma.

'Eleven years.' Nick reached down and stroked the dog. 'Yes, I shall miss old Bob when his time comes.'

'Will you get another?'

'Maybe. I don't like to think about it.'

In the fragile silence that followed Emma wished she had steered the conversation in a different direction. She felt on edge and could tell that Nick too was ill at ease. Might she risk a second glass of wine?

'Why has Jim gone to America?' As if reading her thoughts Nick reached for the bottle and topped up her glass. 'It seems an odd time for his company to call a meeting between Christmas and New Year.'

'I know, but they're planning a major reorganisation and Jim thinks he could be out of a job. They made a big concession letting him transfer back to England after Mum got ill. But there isn't really enough for him to do over here.'

'You think they'll fire him?'

'Maybe not fire him. Jim's good at what he does. But I expect they'll be giving him an ultimatum. Come back to Los Angeles or go and work for someone else.'

'So, you might go back to America after all.'

Emma shook her head. 'No way. I've told Jim that if he decides to return to the States, he goes alone.'

Nick studied her for several seconds. 'But you are happy together, aren't you? I'd always assumed that you were.' He hesitated. 'I'm sorry. I've no right to ask such questions.'

Emma reached for her glass. 'If you're asking whether my marriage has turned out the way I'd hoped, the answer is no. For one thing, I'd expected to have children by now. As to whether I'm happy with Jim, I really can't say. I haven't had that many boyfriends to compare him with.'

Nick rose to his feet. 'I'll just go and check on the meal. It's a casserole so I don't have much to do, apart from serve it.'

Emma got up too and followed him into the kitchen. 'Can I help in some way? At least let me lay the table.'

'All done,' said Nick pointing to a small round table in the corner, covered with a gingham cloth and laid for two, complete with, mats, napkins and water glasses. He stirred the casserole. 'This won't be long now,'

Emma stood with her back to the wall watching him. In his navy cords and button down shirt he looked nothing like the priest who said Mass a week before on Christmas morning.

'You said that you lost your faith twenty years ago, Nick. Did it just happen, or was there an event of some kind that triggered it?'

When Nick didn't answer, she thought she must have broached a sensitive subject. Then he turned to face her. 'No, It was an event that triggered it.'

'May I ask what?'

He sighed and shook his head. 'I suppose I shouldn't be telling you this, but the event was you, Emma.'

'Me?'

He turned away and when he spoke again there was a tremor in his voice. 'You have to bear in mind that, twenty years ago, I was a very raw young priest just out of the seminary. You probably don't remember my first Sunday here, but I do. You were sitting with your mother and brother on the right of the centre aisle, close to the front. I hope you don't mind my saying this to you now, but I was mesmerised. Every time I turned to face the congregation I found my eyes were drawn to you.' He resumed stirring the casserole. 'I'm sorry. Now I've embarrassed you, haven't I.'

Emma came quickly forward and put a hand on his shoulder. 'Nick, you haven't. I'm not at all embarrassed. Because it was the same for me. I fell in love with you that first Sunday too.'

He turned to face her. 'You did?'

'Oh, I know it was just a teenage crush and that love has to be based on a lot more than physical attraction. But, I never got over it. All through university and for a long time after, even in America, all I could think about was you and the next time I'd be home so I could see you again.'

Now there were tears in Nick's eyes as he looked at her. 'Really? You felt the same as I did?'

'Absolutely. I used to fantasise about you endlessly. I knew it was impossible, what with you being a priest, but I never got over my teenage crush. Not even when I married Jim.'

All through this exchange they had been facing one another, just inches apart and for a few electric moments it seemed they might even embrace. But then one or the other, perhaps both, realised it was a line they could not cross and they separated, Nick to attend to the casserole and Emma to the kitchen table where she sat down.

'Here we are.' Nick brought the casserole to the table, followed by dishes of beans and potatoes. 'I suppose I was a late developer,' he said, sitting down. 'As a teenager I wasn't much into girls. But that's no excuse. No one forced me to become a priest.' He handed her a serving spoon. 'Anyway, let's eat.'

For the next hour they talked, sometimes excitedly, sometimes regretfully as they shared their memories and fantasies. Nick told her how, for the three years she was away at university, he had wrestled with his conscience, asking himself whether he should leave the priesthood. He had seen her maybe half a dozen times during that period and each time he looked for a signal that she cared for him as more than just a friend. But she never gave him that signal. Or, if she did, he was too naive and unworldly to recognise it.

'Then you got your degree and I dared to hope you might get a job somewhere not too far away. But you didn't, of course. You went to work for the BBC in London and came home even less often. It was around that time that I went through a very dark period. I was drinking too much, and I even started to look at pornography. I know that sounds shocking, coming from a man of the cloth, but you may as well have the truth.'

'Did you break your vow of celibacy?'

'Once, yes. I went to London and visited a prostitute. Not knowing any better, I took a walk through Soho and went with the first girl who approached me. I came away feeling dirty and miserable, thinking that celibacy might be preferable after all.'

'But you still didn't think of giving up the priesthood?'

'Oh, I thought about it constantly. But giving up my vocation would have been a massive step. There was my congregation to consider. And my bishop, who had placed such faith in me over many years. Then there were my parents, both still terribly affected by the loss of my brother. I knew what leaving the priesthood would do to them. Besides, I had found a lot of reward in my work as a priest. It gave me a sense of purpose and self worth that I'm not sure I would have found elsewhere.'

Nick got up from his chair. 'Why don't you go and sit in front of the fire while I clear up a little and make some coffee.'

Emma got up and walked into the other room, lit now only by the fire. Although she had drunk no more than two glasses of wine, the conversation had been more than a little intoxicating. She wasn't sure whether she was happy or sad to discover that Nick had been nursing a passion for her all these years. She suspected that she would now spend the next twenty years regretting her failure to signal her own feelings more strongly.

'Here we are,' said Nick coming in from the kitchen with a tray of coffee. 'I've just let Bob out. But he'll be scratching at the door any moment.'

'Will he come back and join us by the fire?'

'No. He'll go to his bed. It's way past his bedtime'

She laughed. 'So, we won't even have a canine chaperone to watch over us.'

Nick laughed too. 'We won't. So we had better be on our best behaviour.'

Emma watched him as he poured the coffee. Then she said, 'You know those fantasies you used to have about me...'

'Yes, and have still from time to time.'

'Are they always sexual fantasies?'

'No. Mostly they aren't even particularly romantic. I just imagine myself in an alternative life. One in which I never entered the priesthood, but came here twenty years ago in some job or other and met you and your family by some other means. Then, while you were at Oxford I wrote you long passionate letters.'

'Did we become lovers at any point?'

'Of course.'

'Before or after university?'

'While you were there. You invited me for a weekend and we made love for the first time on some rickety, protesting bed at your digs.'

'And after university, what then? Did I meet Jim and go to live in Los Angeles?'

'No. You stayed in London and I used to come and visit you until, with the blessing of both our families, we got married and had children and lived happily ever after.' Nick smiled. 'Something like that.'

'Only one bit wrong. I was never in digs when I was at Oxford. I was in college the whole time.'

'Thank you for that.. I will adjust my fantasy forthwith.'

Emma was silent for a long time. Then she said, 'Have you ever wondered what happens to fantasies when people get the opportunity to act them out for real?'

'You mean their sexual fantasies?'

'Yes, their sexual fantasies. I mean, does it serve only to destroy what little they had, or does it help them cope better with the lives they have chosen for themselves?'

Nick sighed. 'Years ago I went to see an Alan Bennett play and one line from that play has always stayed with me. 'Whether you do or you don't, you'll probably live to regret it.'

For a long time neither spoke as they gazed into the dying embers of the fire. Then the clock chimed and broke the spell. Emma looked at her watch. 'Oh dear. It's later than I thought. I must go.' She made to get up, but had to steady herself. 'I think our conversation must have gone to my head a little. I'm not sure how I feel.'

Getting up, Nick came over and took her arm. 'Emma, it isn't safe for you to drive home. Why don't I make up a bed for you down here. It won't take me a minute.'

She shook her head. 'No. I can't stay here. What if someone should see me leave in the morning?'

'Not if you stay for breakfast. If you leave around 10.30am who's to know you didn't call round in the morning on Church business? Or you could leave early, around 6.00am while it's still dark. No one would see you then.'

Emma hesitated. 'You're right. I can't possible drive now. If you're sure it's no trouble. Yes, I'll sleep it off for a few hours and leave early. I'll get up at six and go while it's still dark. There's no need for you to get up.'

'Fine. You sit down again and I'll have the bed ready in no time. And don't worry. You won't be disturbed in the night, I promise.'

'She gave him a mischievous smile. 'But what if I should come to you?'

He studied her face for a moment and then he kissed her gently on the lips. 'You won't come to me. You'll stay here like a good girl and go to sleep.'

Chapter Twenty One

Emma sat at a coffee bar waiting for the Los Angeles flight to land. It wasn't due for another twenty minutes, but she had come early in case it touched down ahead of schedule. She had taken more trouble than usual with her appearance today. Instead of her customary daywear of baggy jumper and old jeans she had put on the chiffon tunic top and black leggings that she rejected a week ago for her evening with Nick. Her hair was different too. Instead of the usual ponytail, it was now styled into a fashionable bob with highlights.

She looked up at the screen and saw that Flight 261 had landed. Soon Jim would appear, tousled and tired after his long journey. The meetings had gone well at first. So well in fact that by new year he was preparing to fly home, confident that the London job was secure. Then, just as he was about to leave for the airport, he was called back to HQ for further talks. They had changed their minds. The UK operation was to be closed in favour of expanding into South America. If he agreed to return to Los Angeles, that job was his. If not, they would have to let him go. She could tell over the phone that he was devastated.

Whether you do or you don't you'll probably live to regret it.

It had never been her intention to go upstairs. As they kissed goodnight she was determined to do as Nick said and go straight to bed in front of the fire. But, after a few minutes of lying there, listening as he came out of the bathroom and crossed the landing to his bedroom, the temptation became too hard to resist. She waited another five minutes, then slipped out of bed, put on the dressing gown Nick had provided for her and crept up the stairs. He had left the light on in the bathroom so she could see around her, but which room was he in? She paused and listened. Yes, he was in the front bedroom. She could hear the gentle sound of his breathing. Tiptoeing to the door, she pushed it open enough to see into the room. She pulled it to again. It hadn't occurred to her that he would be in a single bed or that he might be already asleep.

No, she couldn't do it. She mustn't. She wasn't a teenager any more, but a married woman with loyalties and responsibilities. How would she live with herself in the knowledge that she had broken her marriage vows? And not just with any man, but with Father Nick Hennessy, a man highly regarded in the community as well as a close friend of the family. He might be a non believer, but he was still a priest and fully intended to remain so. No, she should resist the temptation. If sex outside marriage was already a mortal sin, how much worse to seduce a priest, a man sworn to celibacy. She might live to regret her decision, but at least she would be able to live with herself, in the knowledge that she had faced down temptation.

Flight 261's baggage was in the hall. Emma got up and walked towards the barrier, pushing herself through the greeters holding up cards. At last a larger group of passengers began to come through, and yes, there was Jim coming into Arrivals, smiling vacantly as he scanned the crowd looking for her.

'Jim, I'm here!' Waving wildly she hurried to the end of the barrier to greet him.

'Hi!' Putting down his case, Jim threw his arms around her and hugged her for a long time. 'My... am I glad to be home.'

She kissed him. 'It's lovely to see you. You've had a miserable time. Was it really awful?'

He shrugged. 'They handled it as well as they knew how. But they'd made up their minds and I could see it from their point of view.'

'Still, you're home now. Come on. We can talk in the car.'

Whether you do or you don't, you'll probably live to regret it

If only it had been like that. If only she had turned away from the temptation, as she had done in her mind a hundred times since New Year. She knew perfectly well what she was doing, even as she crept to his bedside and ran her fingers lightly through his hair to wake him. He sat up with such a start that, for a few seconds, she feared he might be angry with her. But, as she slipped off the dressing gown and stood naked before him, he lifted the duvet for her to climb into the bed beside him.

For a while she was able to luxuriate in the thrill of just being in Nick's arms and feeling the warmth of his body. This was the bliss she had longed for, the fulfilment of all those years of passionate imaginings. But it wasn't long before they both began to realise that a narrow creaking, single bed wasn't the best place for two people to rest in comfort, let alone make love. Nevertheless, they persisted, experimenting with different positions until eventually he managed to penetrate her. In less than a minute it was over. Rolling off her he buried his head in the pillow. Within another minute he was asleep.

For twenty minutes or so she lay beside him, half in and half out of the duvet, wondering whether to wake him again, or return downstairs where at least she would be warm. Eventually she could stand it no longer. Sliding out of bed she picked the dressing gown off the floor and wrapping it round her, returned downstairs to the sofa bed to spend the rest of the night reflecting morosely on what she had done. At 5.00am she got dressed, crept guiltily from the house and walked briskly to her car. She was deeply disappointed. Making love to Nick was no more fulfilling than having sex with Jim.

Yes, she would regret what she had done for the rest of her life. So much so that she decided that she wouldn't see Nick again, but nor did she want to. He was longer a person she could look up to, place on a pedestal, admire from afar. He was just a man like any other, no worse but certainly no better. Were he to leave the Church, perhaps she could admire him more, but he was choosing not to. He would continue with his vocation, he said, in the hope that one day he might find his way back to God. Did she believe that? Or was he just choosing the easy option of staying within the priesthood, where at least he had status, a regular income and a roof over his head. Evidently that was what her mother believed. To her he was a fraud, an imposter. But Emma wasn't so sure.

'You look different somehow.'

Jim had been slumped in his seat for the first part of the journey, but he was sitting up now as they cruised along the M25 towards Amersham,

'Have you done something to your hair?'

Emma smiled. 'Ah, you've noticed at last. Yes. I decided to go to Solihull and let Zoe give me a makeover. I can always change it back if you don't like it.'

'No, it makes you look younger.' He hesitated. 'Sorry. What I mean to say is....'

She laughed. 'You don't have to explain. Zoe said the same thing. Anyway, I decided I needed a change.'

Reaching across, she rested her hand on his. 'By the way, I've been thinking about going back to Los Angeles. I don't much care for it as a place, but we don't have to live in the city, do we?'

Jim looked at her in surprise. 'But I thought you said wild horses wouldn't...'

'I know. I've changed my mind. It was wrong of me to put pressure on you like that. No, we'll go to Los Angeles and when we get there, we'll investigate having IVF.'

'Really. Are you sure that wouldn't be against your conscience.'

'No. I think I can be a good Catholic without agreeing to everything that comes out of the Vatican.'

'Are you sure you don't want to be near your dad?'

'Not any more. Dad's got his own life now.'

'Don't tell me you've even made your peace with Sarah.'

'I have actually. I can't see us becoming bosom buddies. But we had lunch on Monday and yes, I think I can live with the idea of her and Dad being an item.' She looked at him. 'You haven't actually resigned yet, I hope.'

'No. I tried to, but they insisted I think it over. I have until the end of the month to decide.'

Emma smiled. 'Good. Because I thought we might go away for a few days, stay in a nice hotel somewhere. How about Paris?'

Jim laughed. 'You have changed. And not just your appearance. Yes, Paris. I'd like that.'

She squeezed his hand. 'That's settled then. We'll book something when we get home. Let's treat it as our second honeymoon.'

END

If you have enjoyed reading **In Thought, Word and Deed** may we recommend James Parr's other novels, **Deferral of Guilt,** published in 2012 and **Seeds of Doubt,** published in 2015.

Deferral of Guilt

When a tramp is found with massive head wounds close to the property of wealthy retired carpet tycoon Frank Brownhills, the police have no reason to suspect him or his glamorous ex-model wife of involvement. But when they find a trail of blood leading into the garden and Carron Brownhills goes missing, the investigation begins to assume larger dimensions. As detectives Pat O'Donnell and Alex Paterson piece together a story of murder, rape, blackmail and revenge each is pursued by his own private demons. For both have guilty secrets which threaten to overwhelm them even before their investigation is completed.

Deferral **of Guilt** went to number one in Amazon's Crime and General Fiction charts.

Seeds of Doubt

Why would anyone want to murder Susan Linton? The British stage actress was just beginning to make her name in Hollywood when her career was cut cruelly short by a riding accident, leaving her confined to a wheelchair. Yet on the day before Easter she is found dead by her housekeeper with multiple stab wounds. Was this the random act of a drug crazed intruder, or was she murdered by someone she knew? Her former husband perhaps, recently released from prison for underage internet grooming. Or Paul, a devoted fan, but a loner with a long history of mental illness.

As Detective Inspector Steve Straker sets out to find the murderer, he faces a crisis in his own life. He and Emily are not getting on and he suspects she may be having an affair. In the coming days, with pressure mounting both at work and at home, Straker finds that he has to revise several assumptions - about colleagues, about witnesses and most of all, about himself.

Printed in Great Britain
by Amazon